ON the CASE with
HOLMES and WATSON

SHE...IES

...stories of
...Doyle

...Cosson
...Morrow

GRAPHIC UNIVERSE™ • MINNEAPOLIS • NEW YORK

Grateful acknowledgment to Dame Jean Conan Doyle for permission to use the Sherlock Holmes characters created by Sir Arthur Conan Doyle

Graphic Universe™
A division of Lerner Publishing Group, Inc.
241 First Avenue North
Minneapolis, MN 55401 U.S.A.

Website address: www.lernerbooks.com

Library of Congress Cataloging-in-Publication Data

Shaw, Murray.
    Sherlock Holmes and the Redheaded League / adapted by Murray Shaw and M.J. Cosson ; illustrated by Sophie Rohrbach and JT Morrow ; from the original stories by Sir Arthur Conan Doyle.
        p.   cm. — (On the case with Holmes and Watson ; #7)
    Summary: Retold in graphic novel form, Sherlock Holmes comes to the aid of a pawnbroker who has joined a club to earn extra money, but suspects something nefarious is happening in his shop while he is away. Includes a section explaining Holmes's reasoning and the clues he used to solve the mystery.
        ISBN: 978-0-7613-7086-4 (lib. bdg. : alk. paper)
        I. Graphic novels. (1. Graphic novels. 2. Doyle, Arthur Conan, Sir, 1859-1930. Redheaded League—Adaptations. 3. Mystery and detective stories.) I. Cosson, M. J. II. Rohrbach, Sophie, ill. III. Morrow, JT, ill. IV. Doyle, Arthur Conan, Sir, 1859-1930. Redheaded League. V. Title. VI. Title: Redheaded League.
    PZ7.7.S46Sik 2011
    741.5'973—dc22   2010035206

Manufactured in the United States of America
1—BC—7/15/12

The Story of
SHERLOCK HOLMES
the Famous Detective

Sherlock Holmes and his helpful friend Dr. John Watson are fictional characters created by British writer Sir Arthur Conan Doyle. Doyle published his first novel about the pair, *A Study in Scarlet*, in 1887, and it became very successful. Doyle went on to write fifty-six short stories, as well as three more novels about Holmes's adventures—*The Sign of Four* (1890), *The Hound of the Baskervilles* (1902), and *The Valley of Fear* (1915).

Sherlock Holmes and Dr. Watson have become some of the most famous book characters of all time. Holmes spent most of his time solving mysteries, but he also had a wide array of hobbies, such as playing the violin, boxing, and sword fighting. Watson, a retired army doctor, met Holmes through a mutual friend when Holmes was looking for a roommate. Watson lived with Holmes for several years at 221B Baker Street before marrying and moving out. However, after his marriage, Watson continued to assist Holmes with his cases.

The original versions of the Sherlock Holmes stories are still printed, and many have been made into movies and television shows. Readers continue to be impressed by Holmes's detective methods of observation and scientific reason.

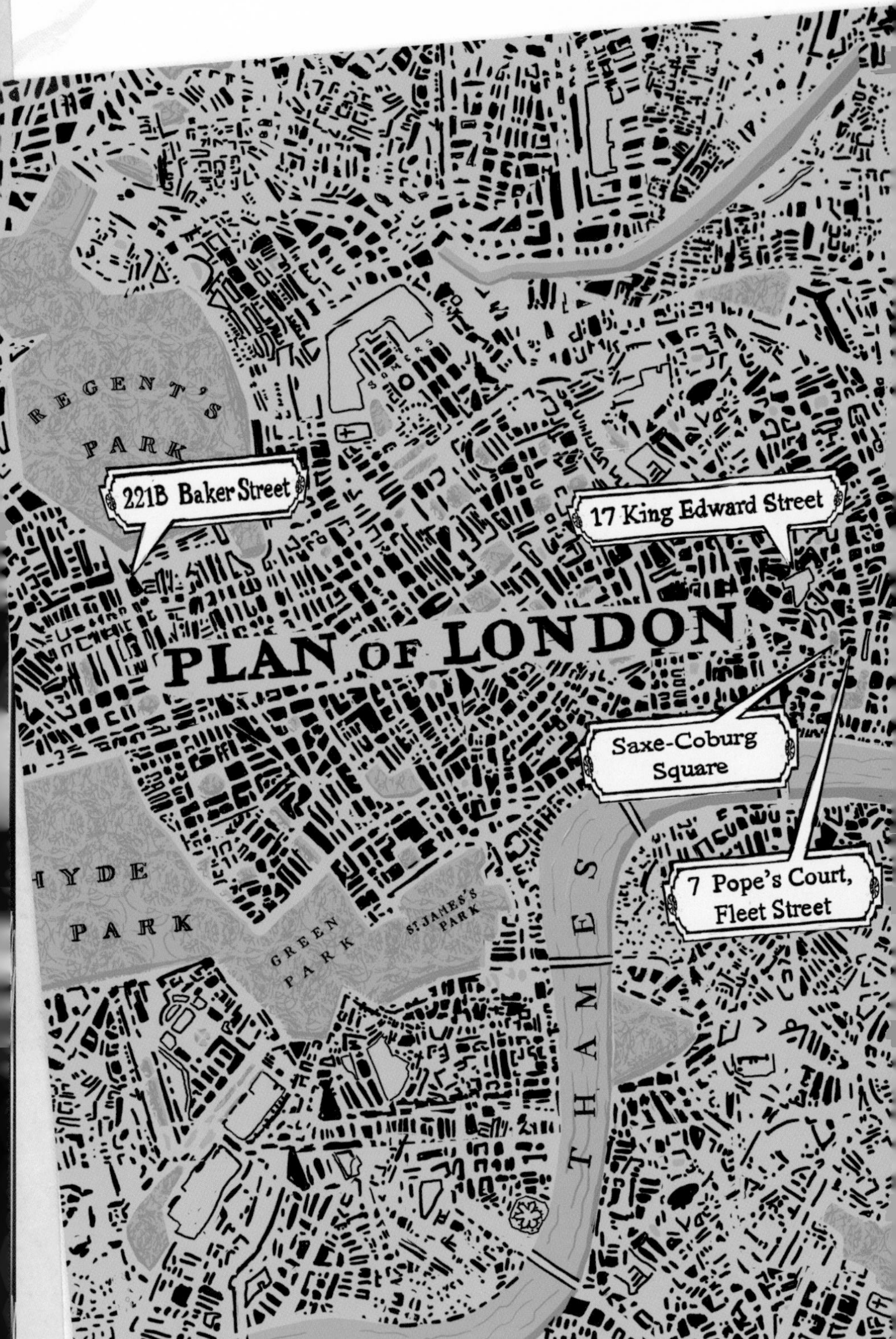

PLAN OF LONDON
REGENT'S PARK
221B Baker Street
SOMERS
17 King Edward Street
Saxe-Coburg Square
7 Pope's Court, Fleet Street
HYDE PARK
GREEN PARK
ST. JAMES'S PARK
THAMES

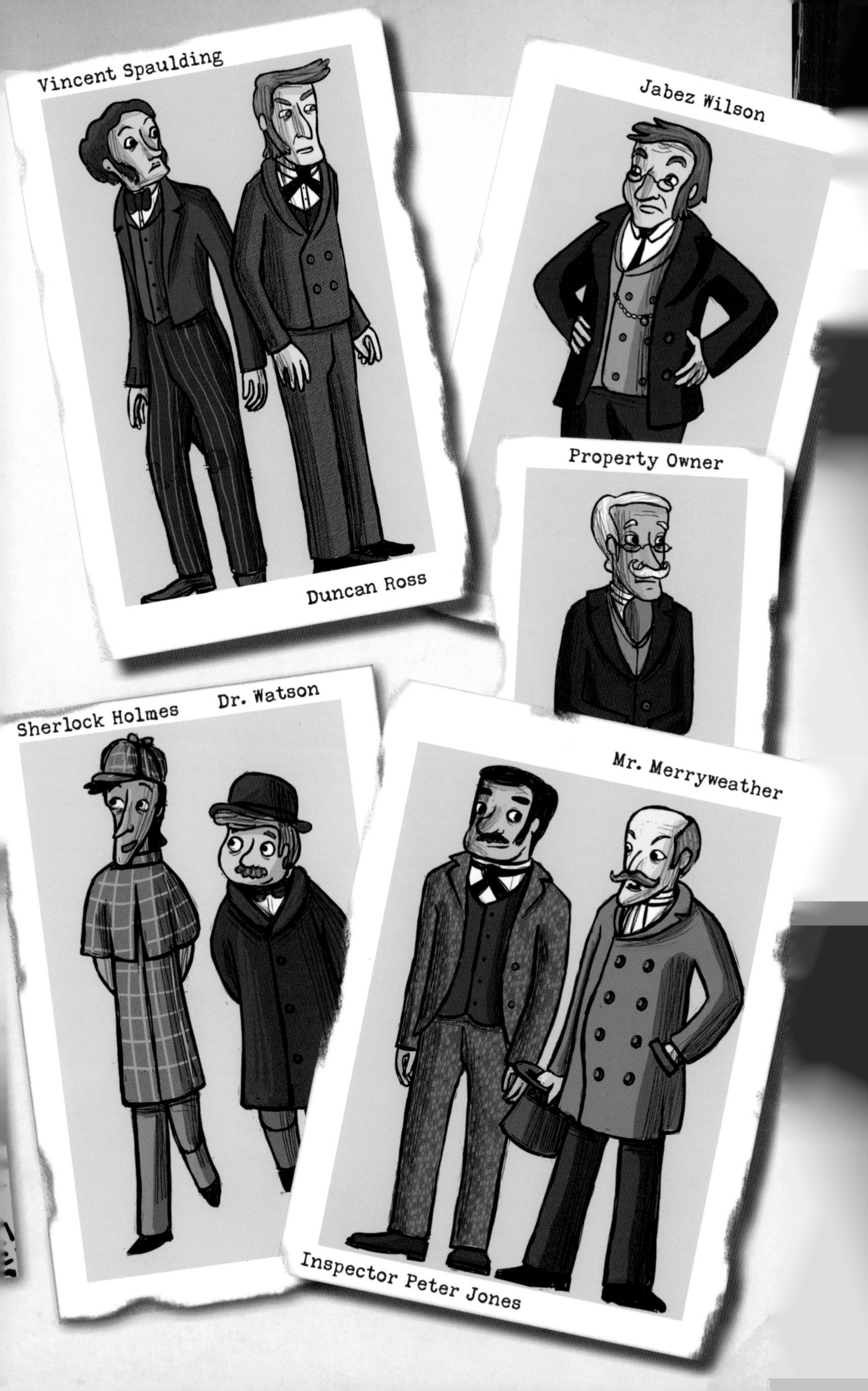
Vincent Spaulding
Duncan Ross
Jabez Wilson
Property Owner
Sherlock Holmes
Dr. Watson
Mr. Merryweather
Inspector Peter Jones

From the Desk of
John H. Watson, M.D.

My name is Dr. John H. Watson. For several years, I have been assisting my friend, Sherlock Holmes, in solving mysteries throughout the bustling city of London and beyond. Holmes is a peculiar man—always questioning and reasoning his way through various problems. But when I first met him in 1878, I was immediately intrigued by his oddities.

Holmes has always been more daring than I, and his logical deduction never ceases to amaze me. I have begun writing down all of the adventures I have with Holmes. This is one of those stories.

Sincerely,

Dr. Watson

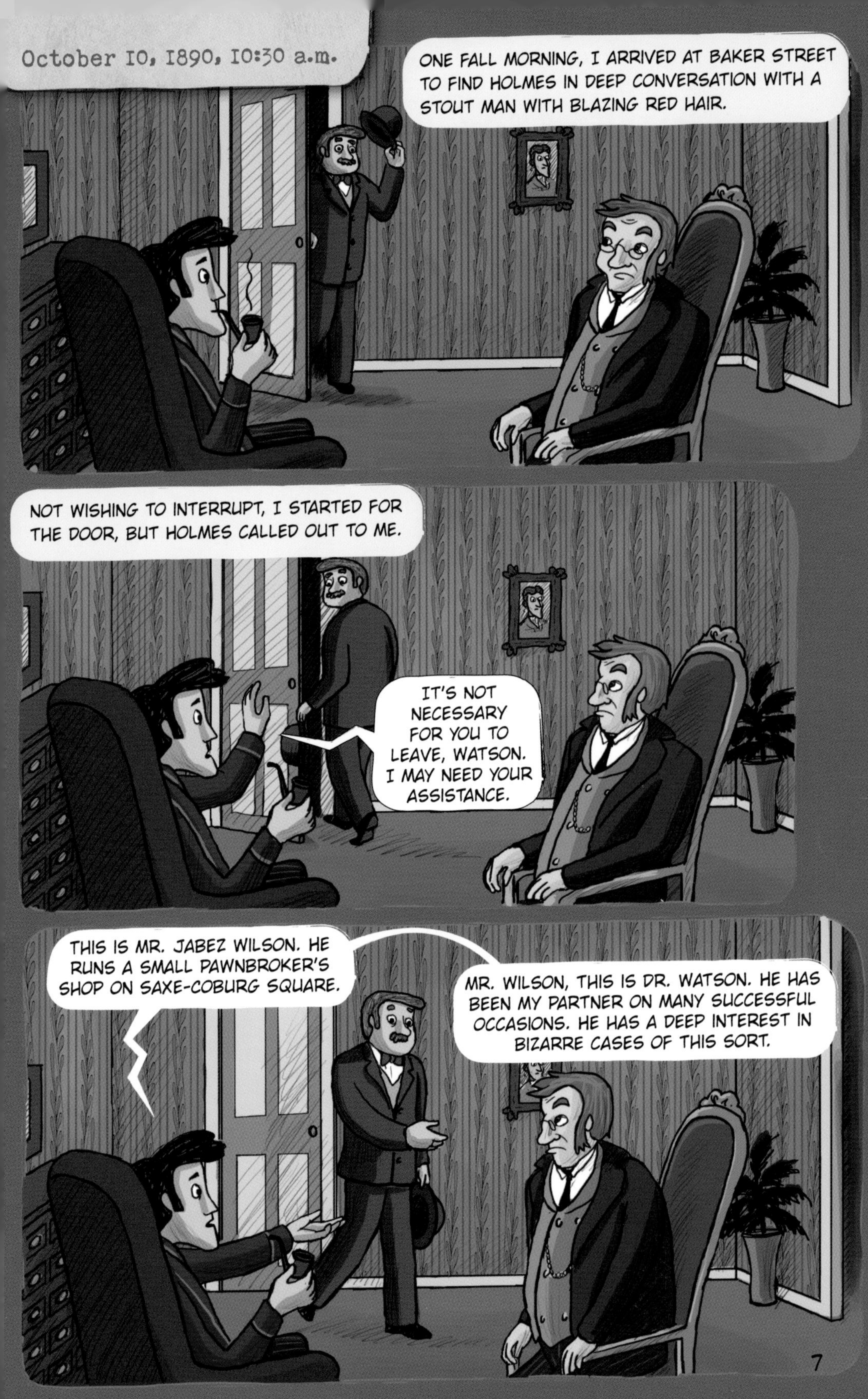
October 10, 1890, 10:30 a.m.
ONE FALL MORNING, I ARRIVED AT BAKER STREET TO FIND HOLMES IN DEEP CONVERSATION WITH A STOUT MAN WITH BLAZING RED HAIR.
NOT WISHING TO INTERRUPT, I STARTED FOR THE DOOR, BUT HOLMES CALLED OUT TO ME.
IT'S NOT NECESSARY FOR YOU TO LEAVE, WATSON. I MAY NEED YOUR ASSISTANCE.
THIS IS MR. JABEZ WILSON. HE RUNS A SMALL PAWNBROKER'S SHOP ON SAXE-COBURG SQUARE.
MR. WILSON, THIS IS DR. WATSON. HE HAS BEEN MY PARTNER ON MANY SUCCESSFUL OCCASIONS. HE HAS A DEEP INTEREST IN BIZARRE CASES OF THIS SORT.

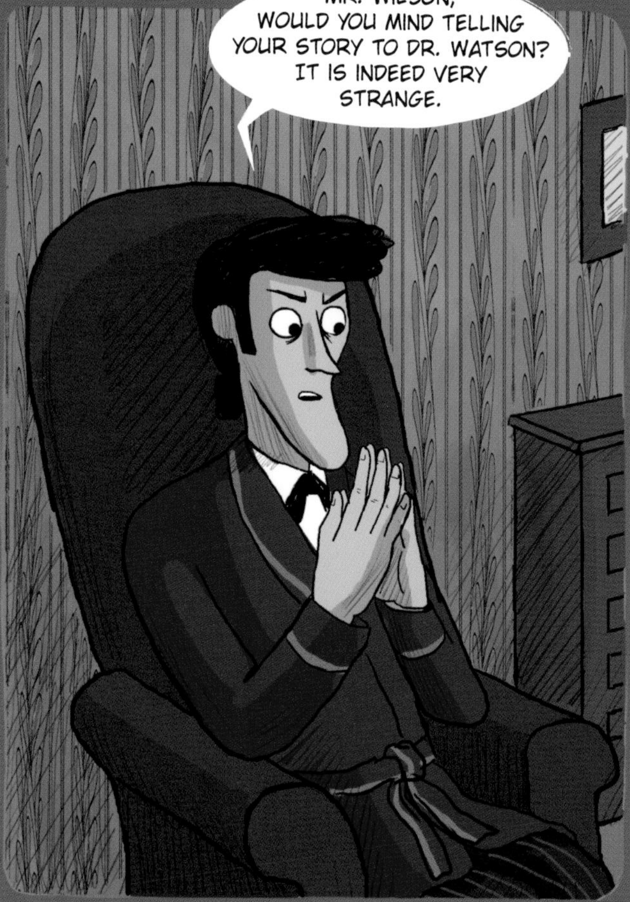
MR. WILSON, WOULD YOU MIND TELLING YOUR STORY TO DR. WATSON? IT IS INDEED VERY STRANGE.

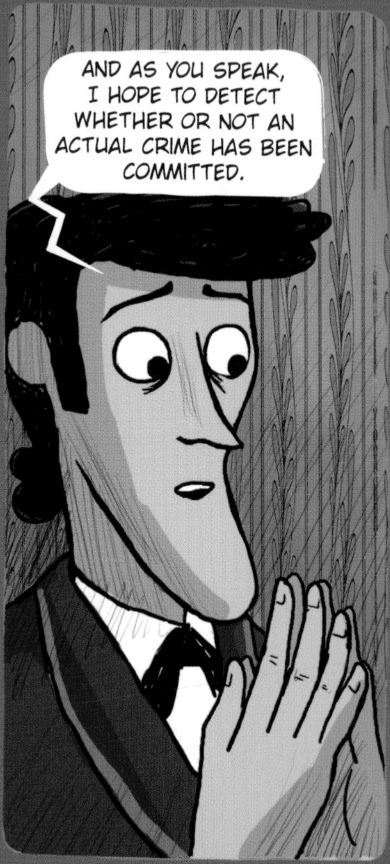
AND AS YOU SPEAK, I HOPE TO DETECT WHETHER OR NOT AN ACTUAL CRIME HAS BEEN COMMITTED.

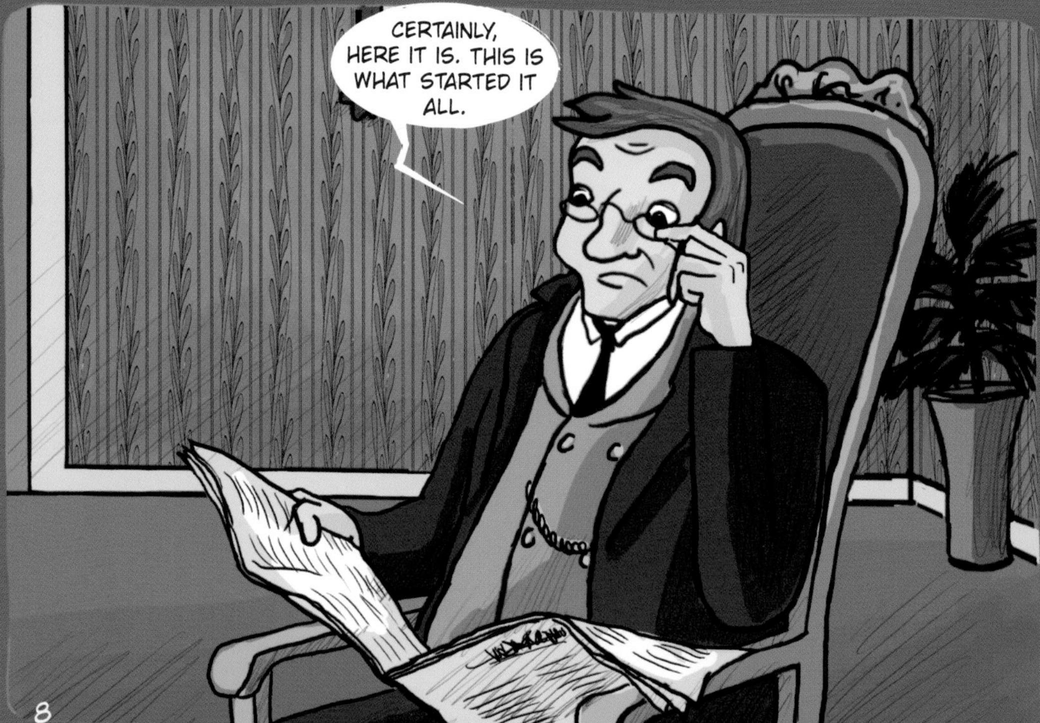
CERTAINLY, HERE IT IS. THIS IS WHAT STARTED IT ALL.

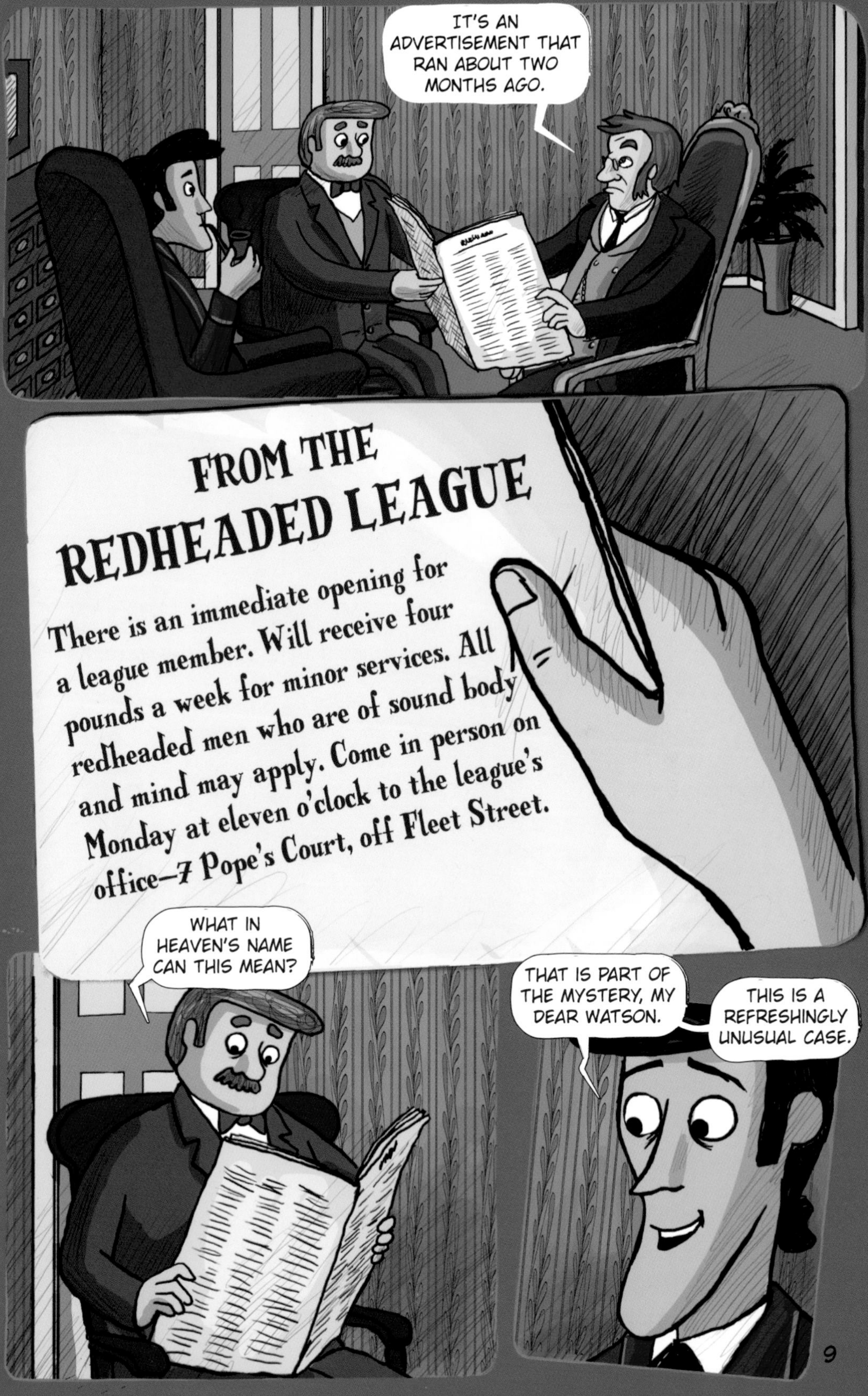
IT'S AN ADVERTISEMENT THAT RAN ABOUT TWO MONTHS AGO.
FROM THE REDHEADED LEAGUE
There is an immediate opening for a league member. Will receive four pounds a week for minor services. All redheaded men who are of sound body and mind may apply. Come in person on Monday at eleven o'clock to the league's office—7 Pope's Court, off Fleet Street.
WHAT IN HEAVEN'S NAME CAN THIS MEAN?
THAT IS PART OF THE MYSTERY, MY DEAR WATSON.
THIS IS A REFRESHINGLY UNUSUAL CASE.

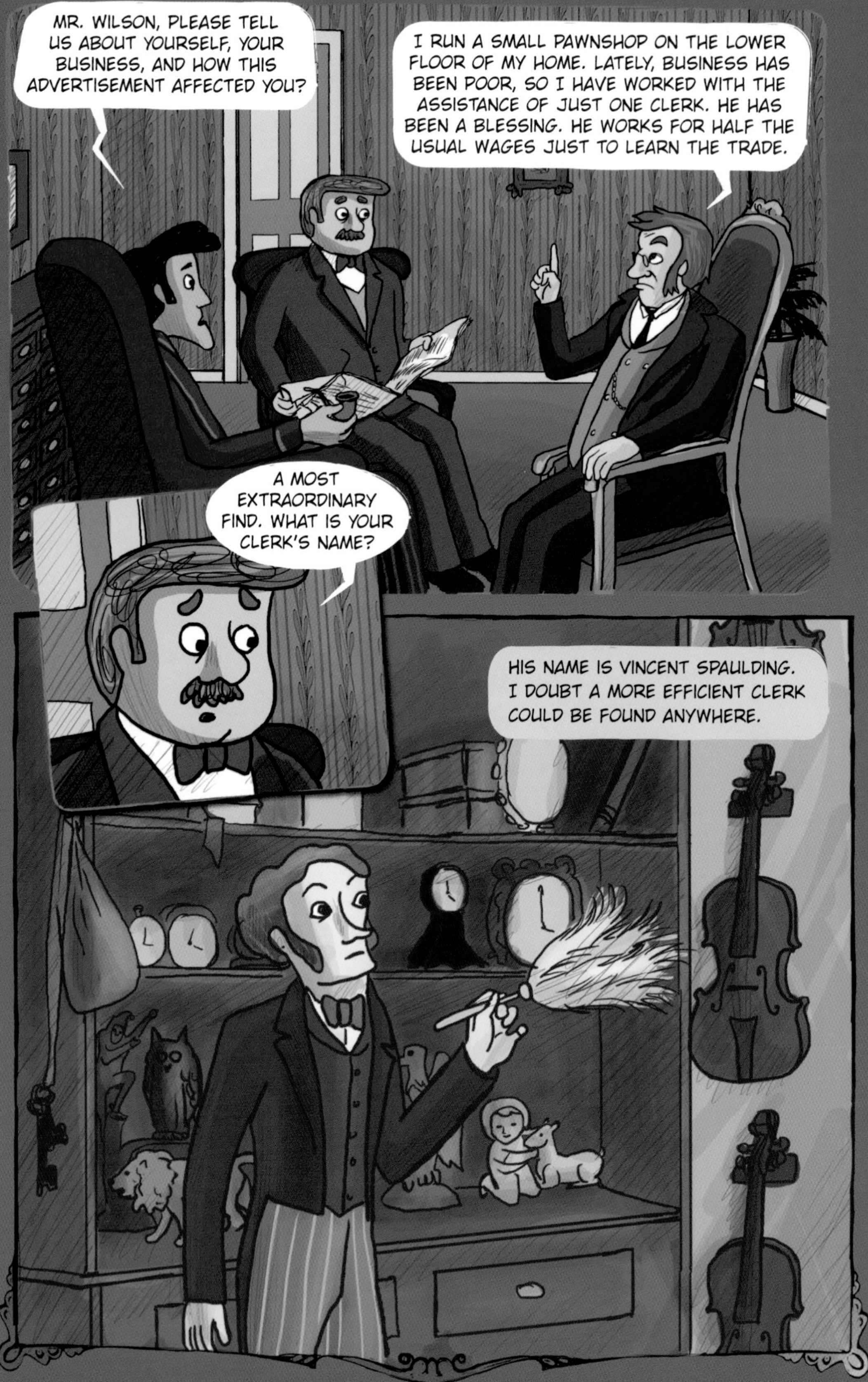
MR. WILSON, PLEASE TELL US ABOUT YOURSELF, YOUR BUSINESS, AND HOW THIS ADVERTISEMENT AFFECTED YOU?
I RUN A SMALL PAWNSHOP ON THE LOWER FLOOR OF MY HOME. LATELY, BUSINESS HAS BEEN POOR, SO I HAVE WORKED WITH THE ASSISTANCE OF JUST ONE CLERK. HE HAS BEEN A BLESSING. HE WORKS FOR HALF THE USUAL WAGES JUST TO LEARN THE TRADE.
A MOST EXTRAORDINARY FIND. WHAT IS YOUR CLERK'S NAME?
HIS NAME IS VINCENT SPAULDING. I DOUBT A MORE EFFICIENT CLERK COULD BE FOUND ANYWHERE.

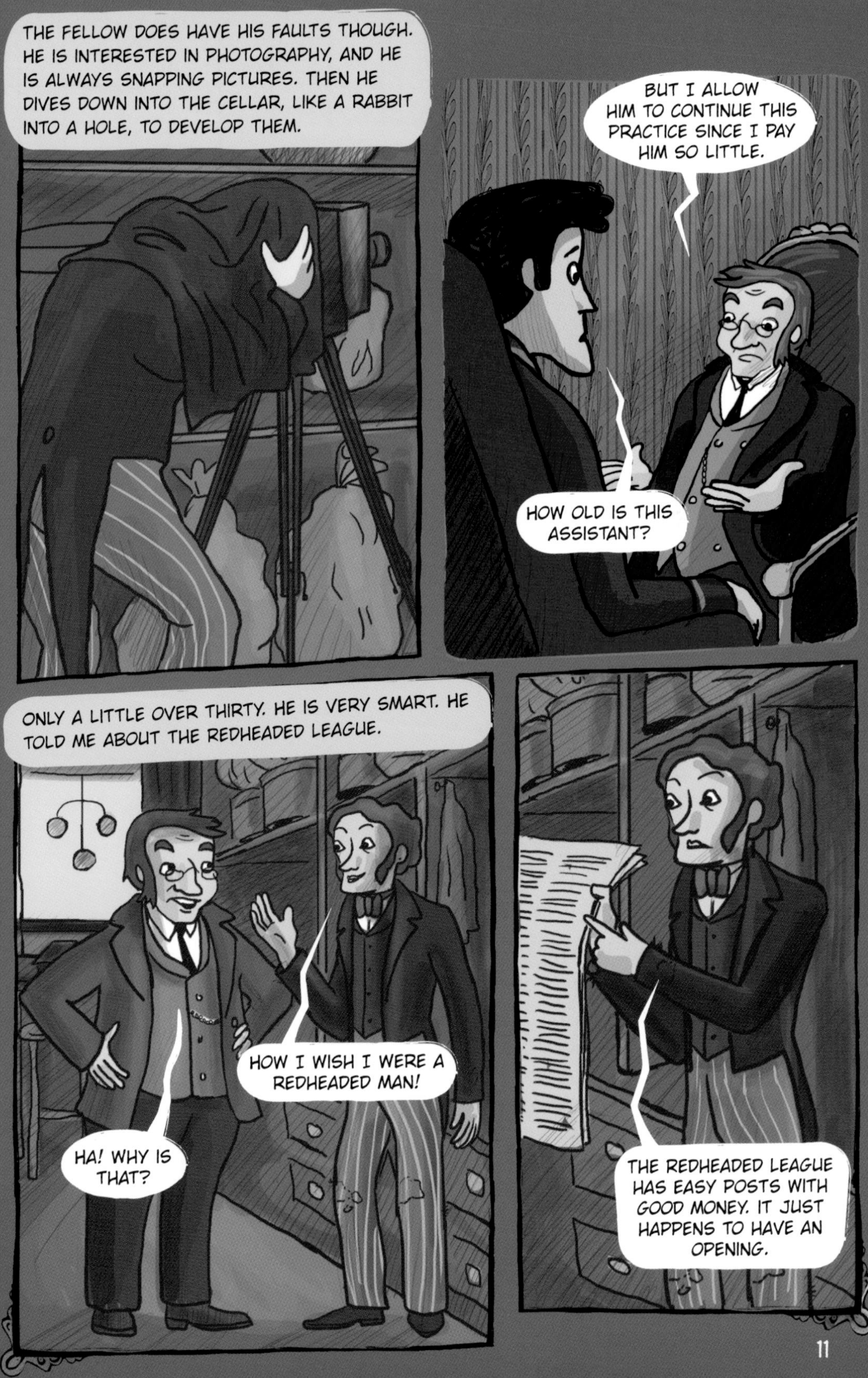
THE FELLOW DOES HAVE HIS FAULTS THOUGH. HE IS INTERESTED IN PHOTOGRAPHY, AND HE IS ALWAYS SNAPPING PICTURES. THEN HE DIVES DOWN INTO THE CELLAR, LIKE A RABBIT INTO A HOLE, TO DEVELOP THEM.
BUT I ALLOW HIM TO CONTINUE THIS PRACTICE SINCE I PAY HIM SO LITTLE.
HOW OLD IS THIS ASSISTANT?
ONLY A LITTLE OVER THIRTY. HE IS VERY SMART. HE TOLD ME ABOUT THE REDHEADED LEAGUE.
HOW I WISH I WERE A REDHEADED MAN!
HA! WHY IS THAT?
THE REDHEADED LEAGUE HAS EASY POSTS WITH GOOD MONEY. IT JUST HAPPENS TO HAVE AN OPENING.

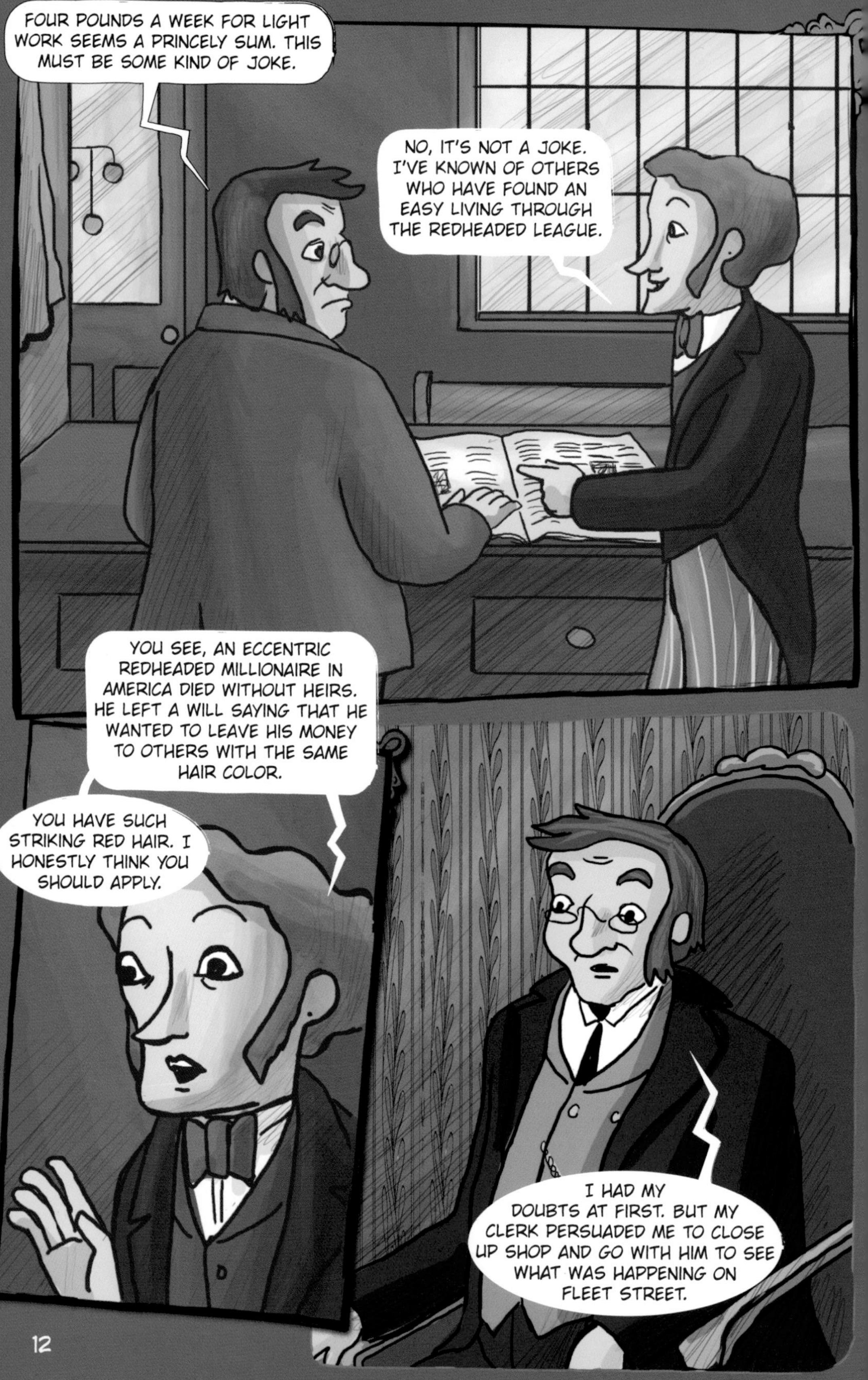
FOUR POUNDS A WEEK FOR LIGHT WORK SEEMS A PRINCELY SUM. THIS MUST BE SOME KIND OF JOKE.
NO, IT'S NOT A JOKE. I'VE KNOWN OF OTHERS WHO HAVE FOUND AN EASY LIVING THROUGH THE REDHEADED LEAGUE.
YOU SEE, AN ECCENTRIC REDHEADED MILLIONAIRE IN AMERICA DIED WITHOUT HEIRS. HE LEFT A WILL SAYING THAT HE WANTED TO LEAVE HIS MONEY TO OTHERS WITH THE SAME HAIR COLOR.
YOU HAVE SUCH STRIKING RED HAIR. I HONESTLY THINK YOU SHOULD APPLY.
I HAD MY DOUBTS AT FIRST. BUT MY CLERK PERSUADED ME TO CLOSE UP SHOP AND GO WITH HIM TO SEE WHAT WAS HAPPENING ON FLEET STREET.

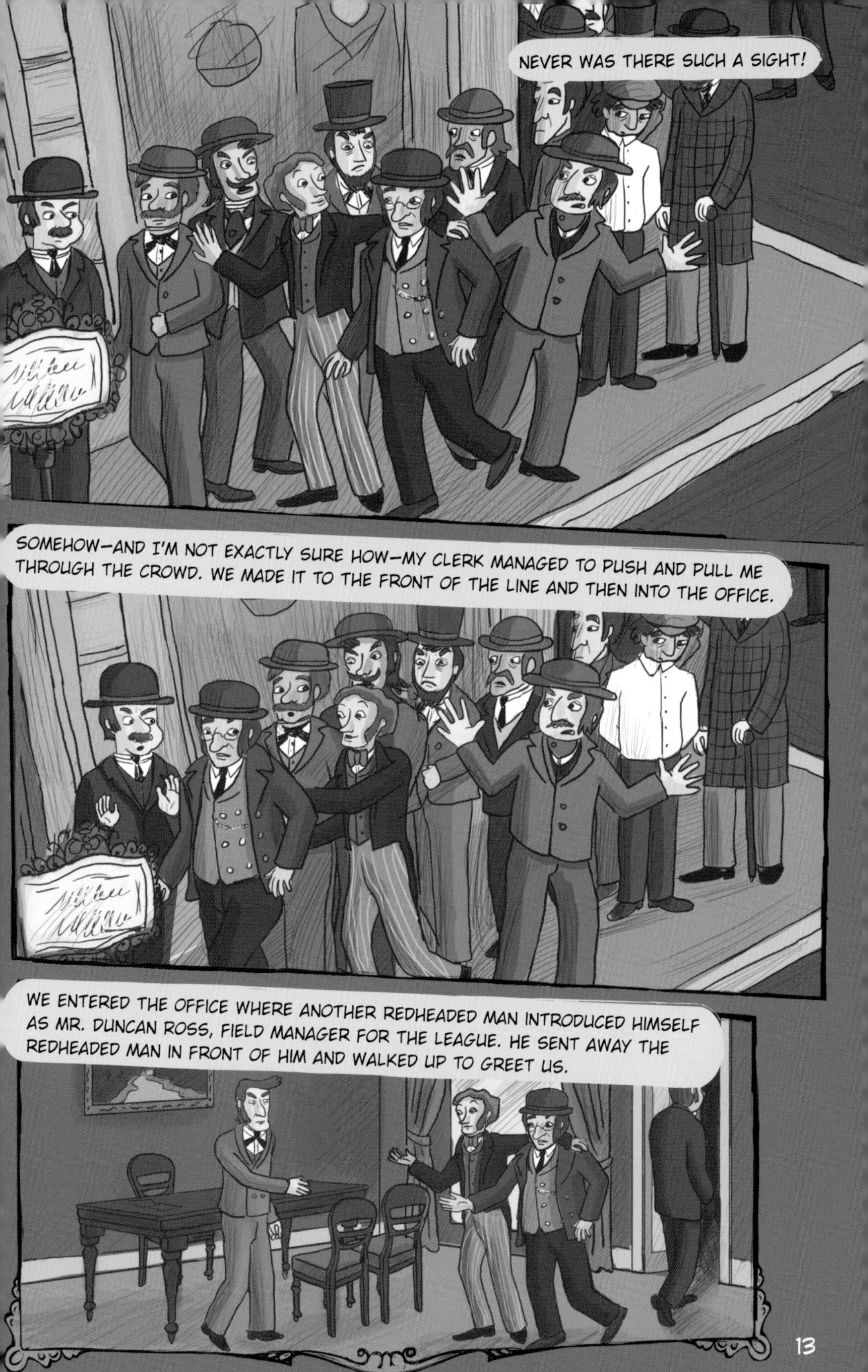
NEVER WAS THERE SUCH A SIGHT!
SOMEHOW—AND I'M NOT EXACTLY SURE HOW—MY CLERK MANAGED TO PUSH AND PULL ME THROUGH THE CROWD. WE MADE IT TO THE FRONT OF THE LINE AND THEN INTO THE OFFICE.
WE ENTERED THE OFFICE WHERE ANOTHER REDHEADED MAN INTRODUCED HIMSELF AS MR. DUNCAN ROSS, FIELD MANAGER FOR THE LEAGUE. HE SENT AWAY THE REDHEADED MAN IN FRONT OF HIM AND WALKED UP TO GREET US.

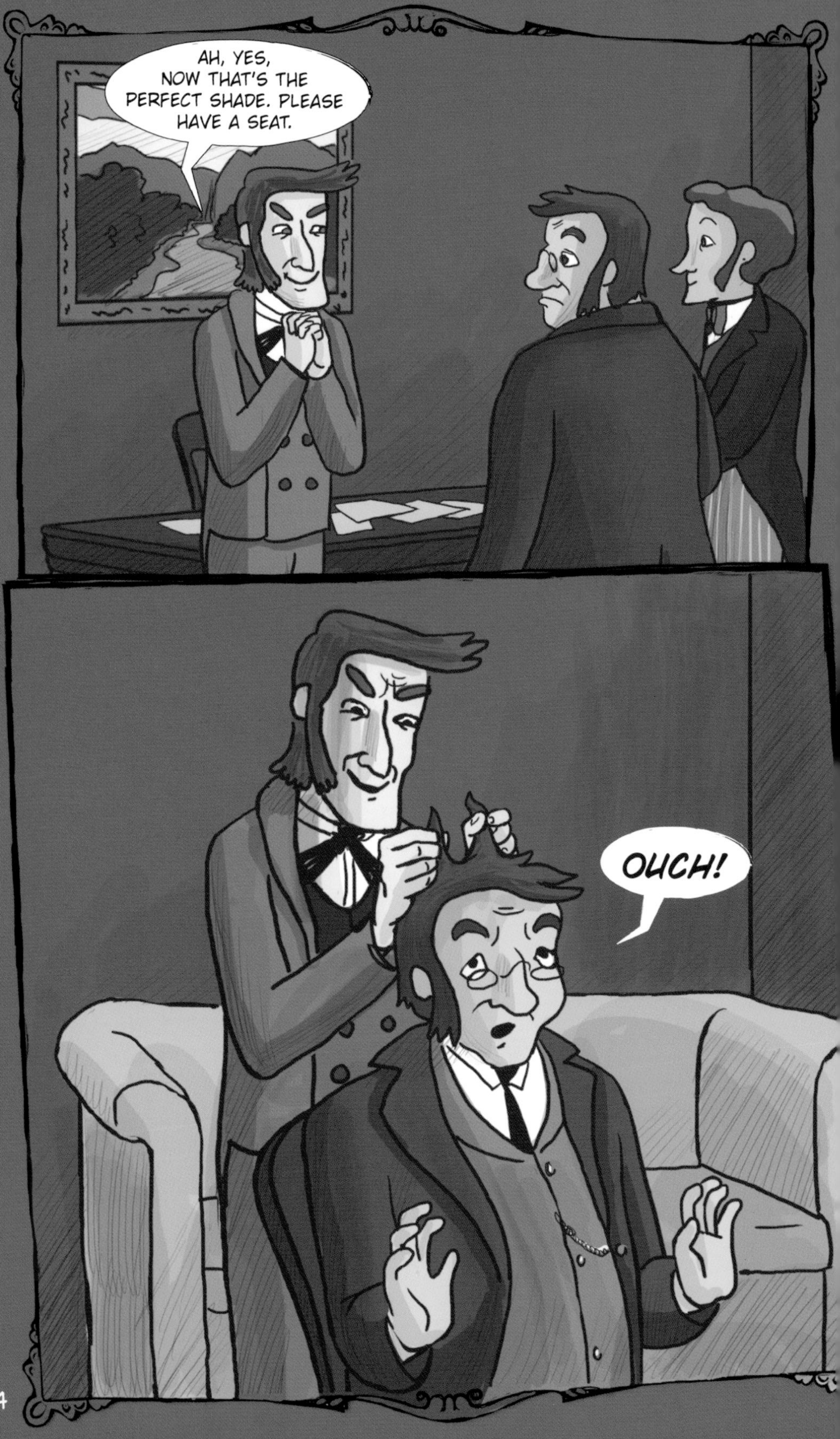
AH, YES, NOW THAT'S THE PERFECT SHADE. PLEASE HAVE A SEAT.
OUCH!

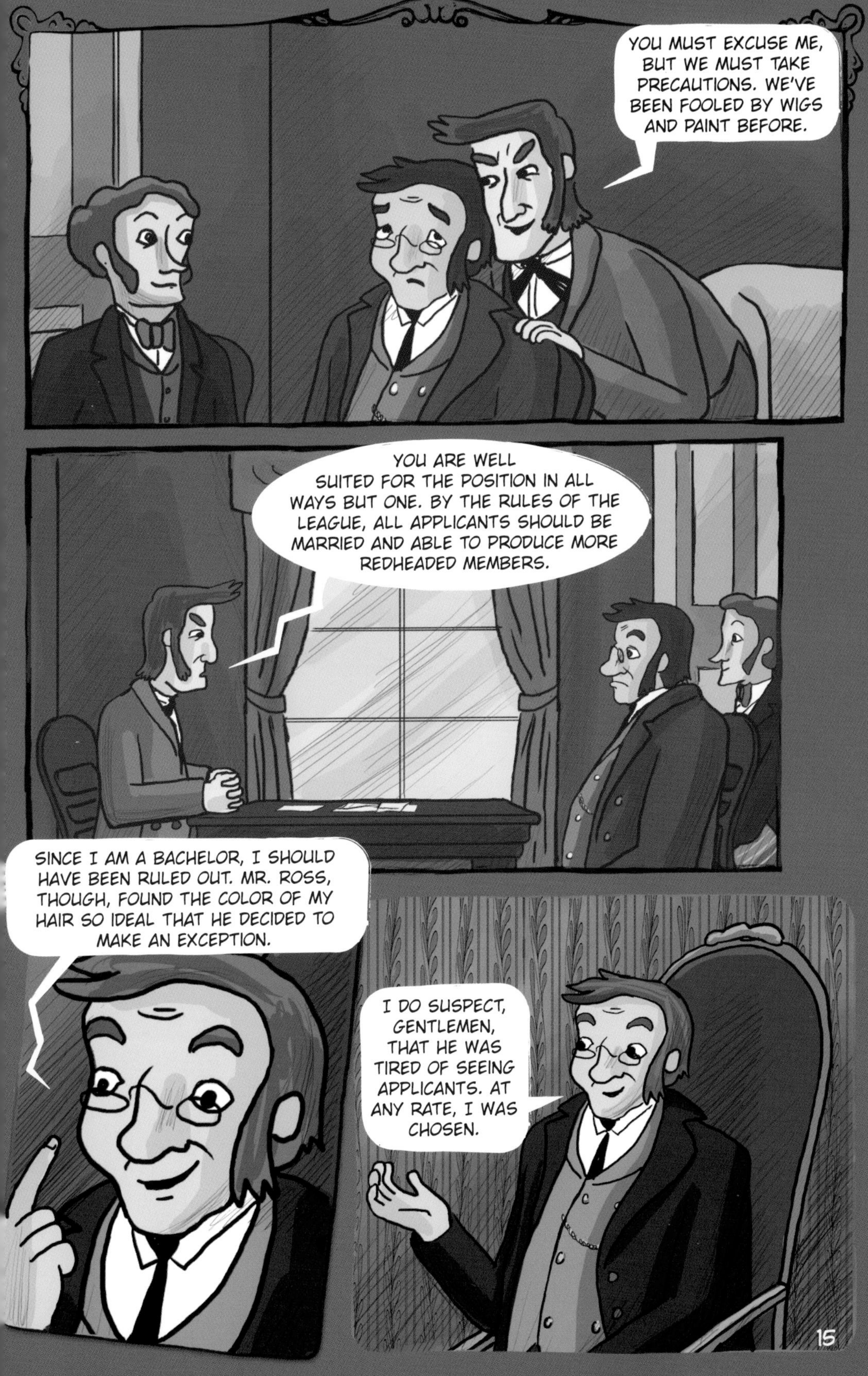

YOU MUST EXCUSE ME, BUT WE MUST TAKE PRECAUTIONS. WE'VE BEEN FOOLED BY WIGS AND PAINT BEFORE.
YOU ARE WELL SUITED FOR THE POSITION IN ALL WAYS BUT ONE. BY THE RULES OF THE LEAGUE, ALL APPLICANTS SHOULD BE MARRIED AND ABLE TO PRODUCE MORE REDHEADED MEMBERS.
SINCE I AM A BACHELOR, I SHOULD HAVE BEEN RULED OUT. MR. ROSS, THOUGH, FOUND THE COLOR OF MY HAIR SO IDEAL THAT HE DECIDED TO MAKE AN EXCEPTION.
I DO SUSPECT, GENTLEMEN, THAT HE WAS TIRED OF SEEING APPLICANTS. AT ANY RATE, I WAS CHOSEN.

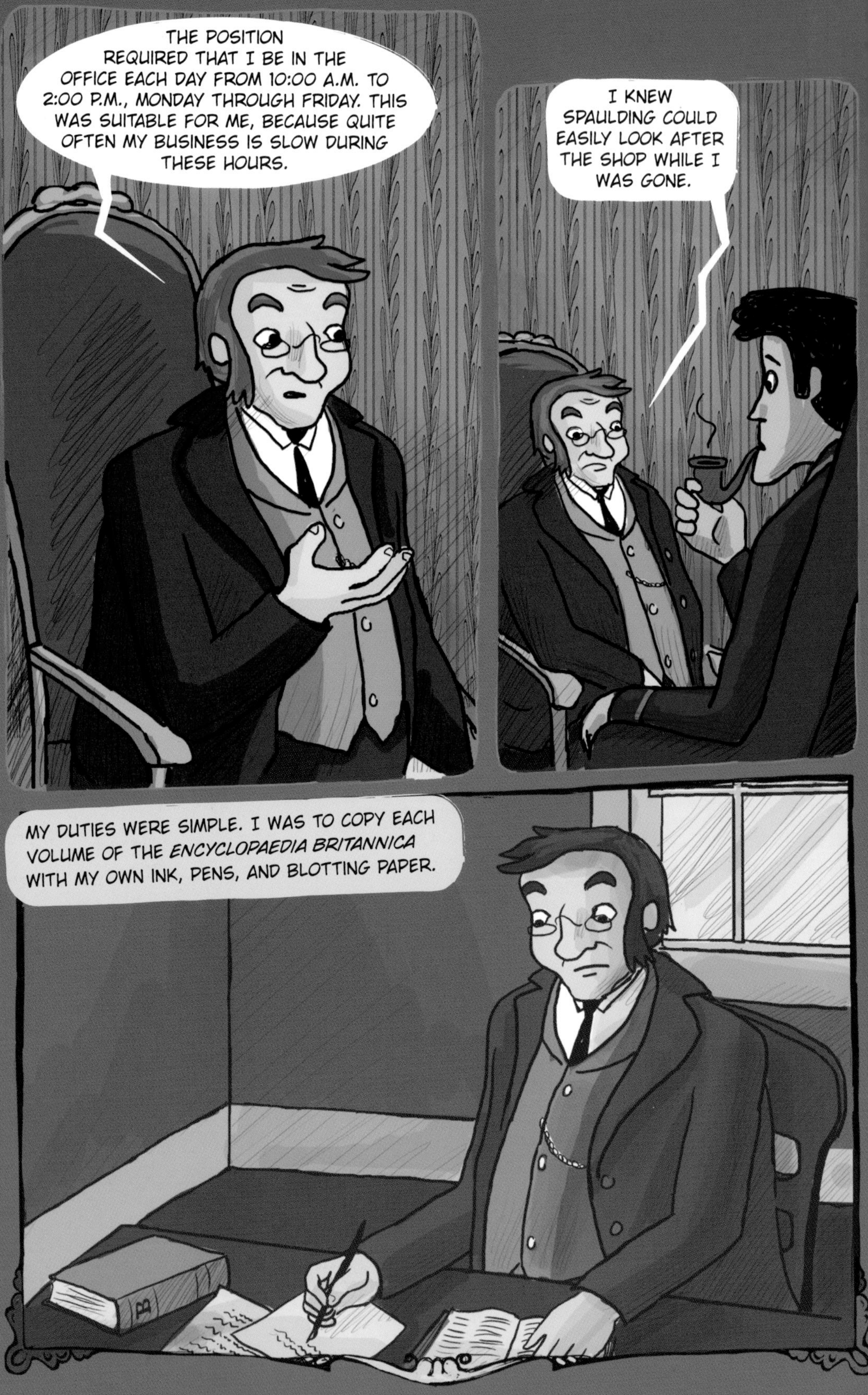
THE POSITION REQUIRED THAT I BE IN THE OFFICE EACH DAY FROM 10:00 A.M. TO 2:00 P.M., MONDAY THROUGH FRIDAY. THIS WAS SUITABLE FOR ME, BECAUSE QUITE OFTEN MY BUSINESS IS SLOW DURING THESE HOURS.
I KNEW SPAULDING COULD EASILY LOOK AFTER THE SHOP WHILE I WAS GONE.
MY DUTIES WERE SIMPLE. I WAS TO COPY EACH VOLUME OF THE *ENCYCLOPAEDIA BRITANNICA* WITH MY OWN INK, PENS, AND BLOTTING PAPER.

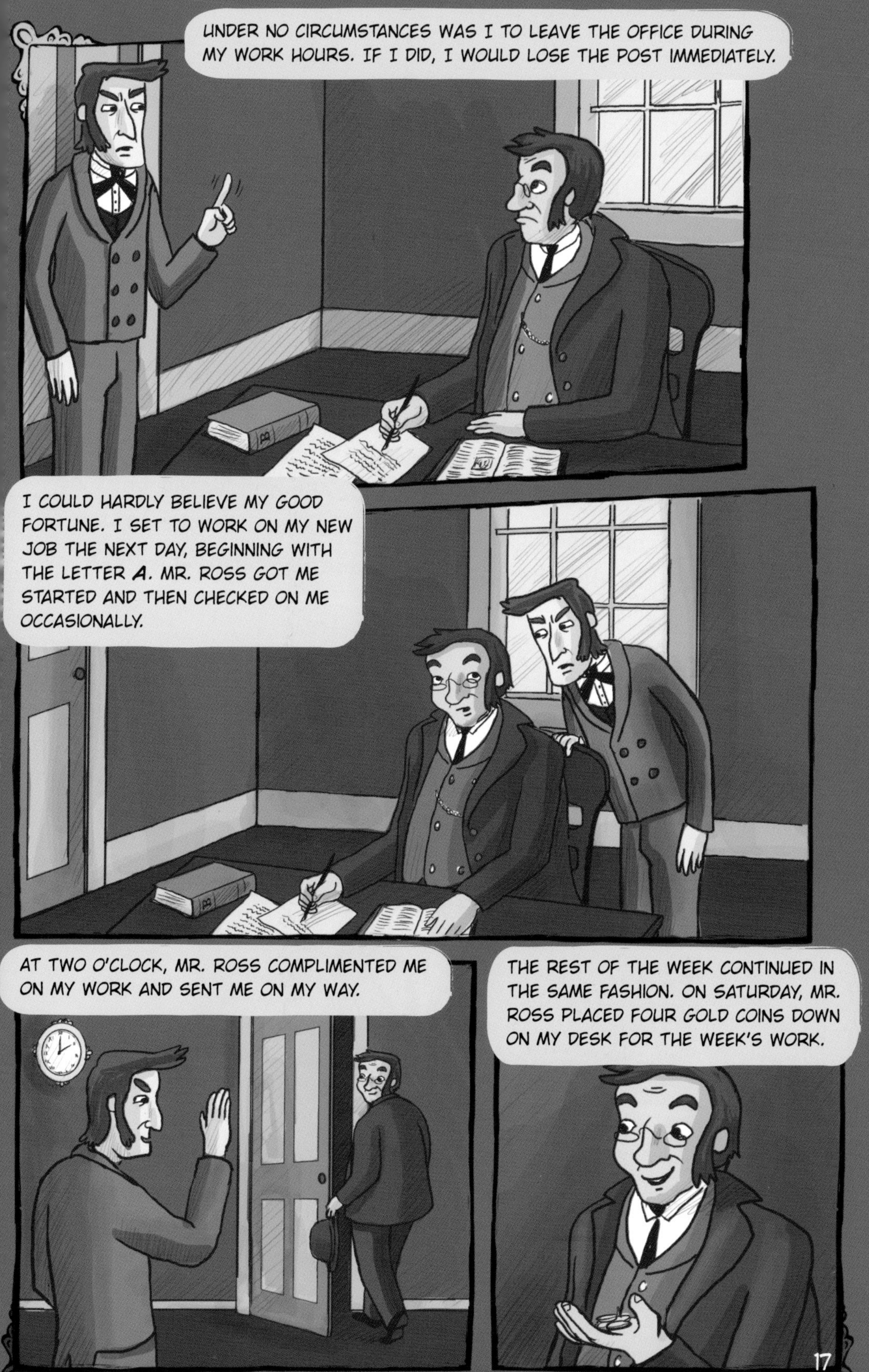
UNDER NO CIRCUMSTANCES WAS I TO LEAVE THE OFFICE DURING MY WORK HOURS. IF I DID, I WOULD LOSE THE POST IMMEDIATELY.
I COULD HARDLY BELIEVE MY GOOD FORTUNE. I SET TO WORK ON MY NEW JOB THE NEXT DAY, BEGINNING WITH THE LETTER A. MR. ROSS GOT ME STARTED AND THEN CHECKED ON ME OCCASIONALLY.
AT TWO O'CLOCK, MR. ROSS COMPLIMENTED ME ON MY WORK AND SENT ME ON MY WAY.
THE REST OF THE WEEK CONTINUED IN THE SAME FASHION. ON SATURDAY, MR. ROSS PLACED FOUR GOLD COINS DOWN ON MY DESK FOR THE WEEK'S WORK.

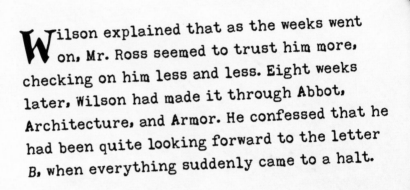

Wilson explained that as the weeks went on, Mr. Ross seemed to trust him more, checking on him less and less. Eight weeks later, Wilson had made it through Abbot, Architecture, and Armor. He confessed that he had been quite looking forward to the letter B, when everything suddenly came to a halt.

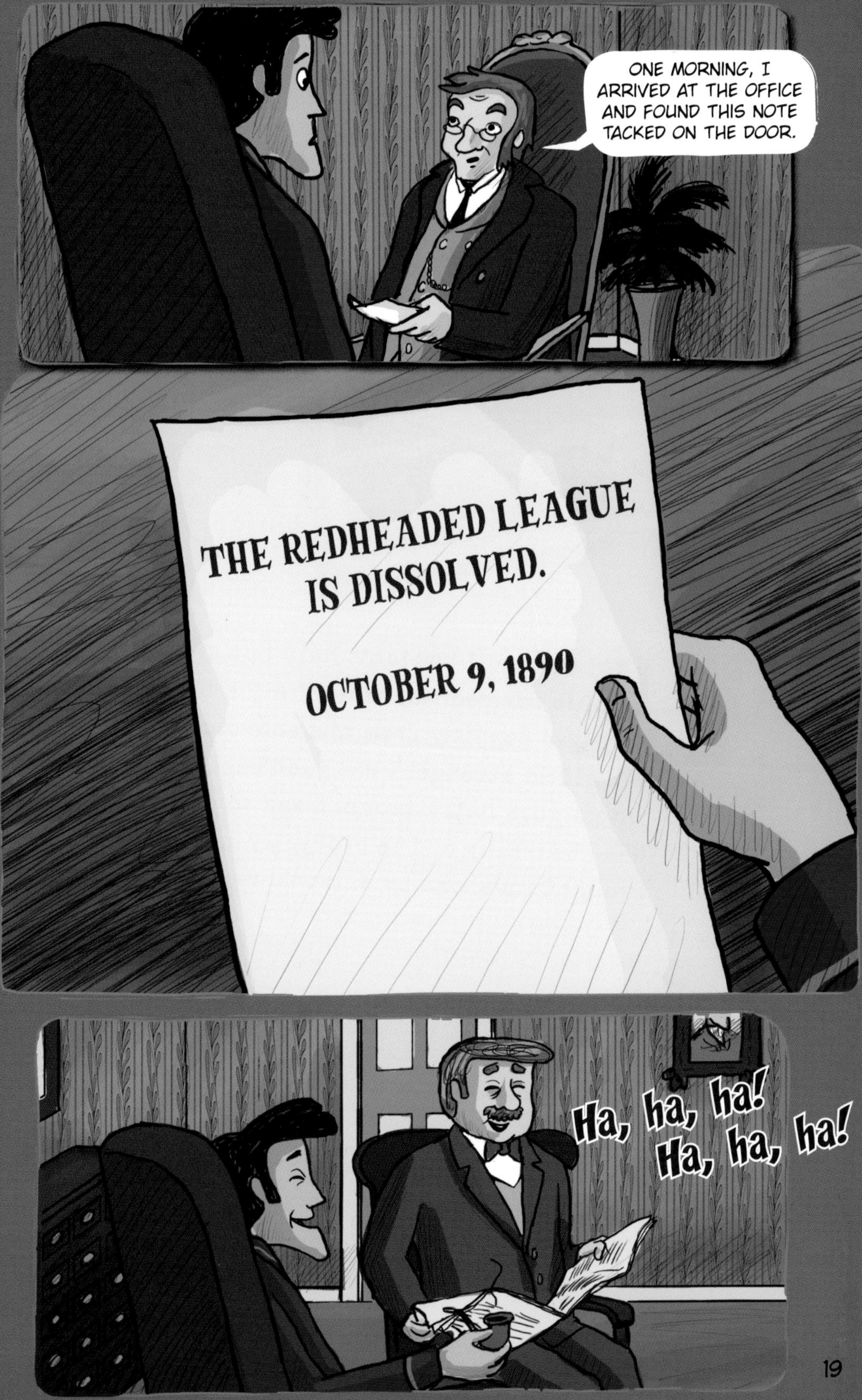
ONE MORNING, I ARRIVED AT THE OFFICE AND FOUND THIS NOTE TACKED ON THE DOOR.
THE REDHEADED LEAGUE IS DISSOLVED.
OCTOBER 9, 1890
Ha, ha, ha! Ha, ha, ha!

Holmes and I couldn't help but chuckle. A club for redheaded men? A job that only involved copying from the encyclopedia? It was all so strange! I was just beginning to roll into a good belly laugh. I was so struck by the absurdity of the story. My laughter was brought up short by Wilson's next words.

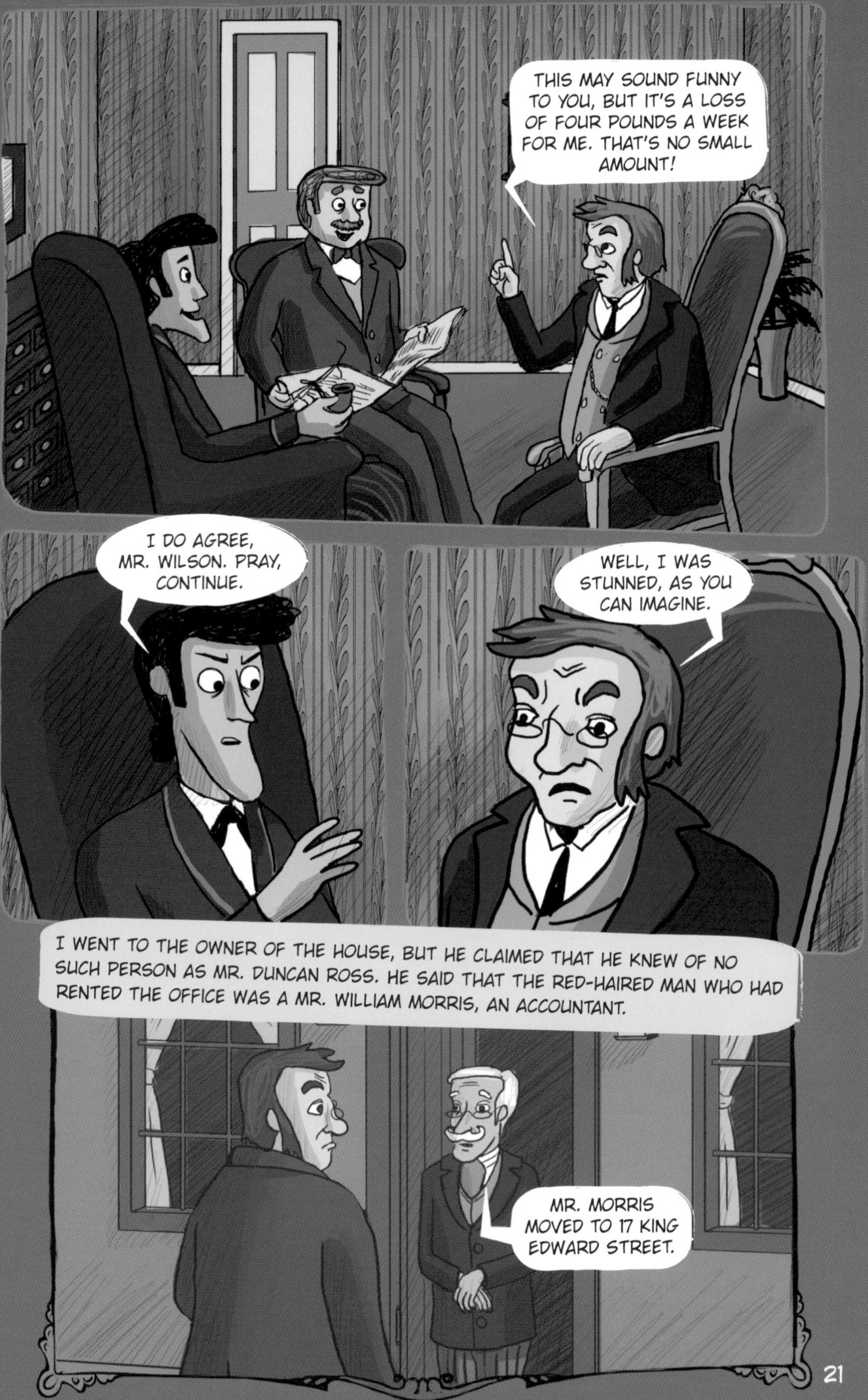

THIS MAY SOUND FUNNY TO YOU, BUT IT'S A LOSS OF FOUR POUNDS A WEEK FOR ME. THAT'S NO SMALL AMOUNT!
I DO AGREE, MR. WILSON. PRAY, CONTINUE.
WELL, I WAS STUNNED, AS YOU CAN IMAGINE.
I WENT TO THE OWNER OF THE HOUSE, BUT HE CLAIMED THAT HE KNEW OF NO SUCH PERSON AS MR. DUNCAN ROSS. HE SAID THAT THE RED-HAIRED MAN WHO HAD RENTED THE OFFICE WAS A MR. WILLIAM MORRIS, AN ACCOUNTANT.
MR. MORRIS MOVED TO 17 KING EDWARD STREET.

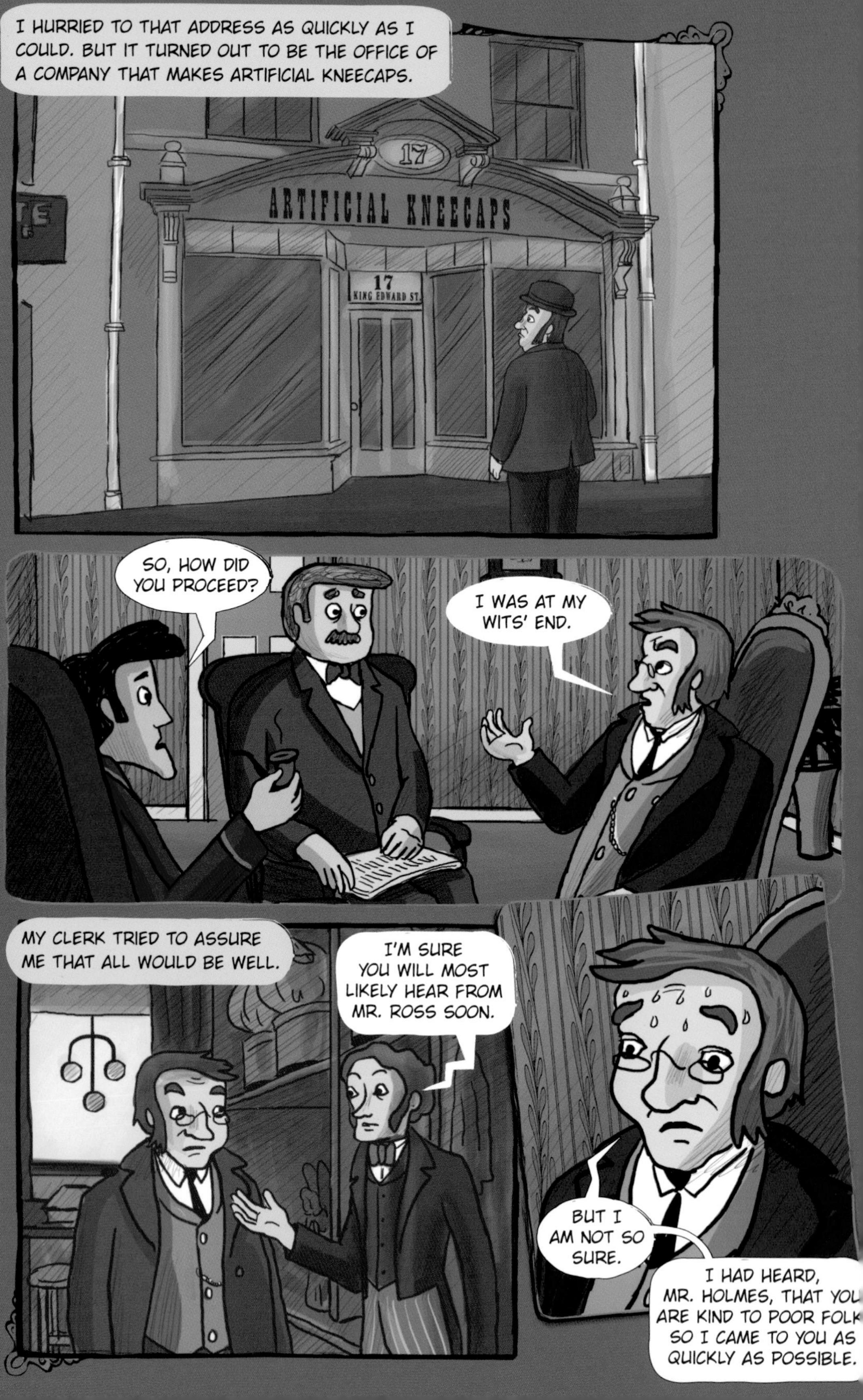
I HURRIED TO THAT ADDRESS AS QUICKLY AS I COULD. BUT IT TURNED OUT TO BE THE OFFICE OF A COMPANY THAT MAKES ARTIFICIAL KNEECAPS.
17
ARTIFICIAL KNEECAPS
17 KING EDWARD ST.
SO, HOW DID YOU PROCEED?
I WAS AT MY WITS' END.
MY CLERK TRIED TO ASSURE ME THAT ALL WOULD BE WELL.
I'M SURE YOU WILL MOST LIKELY HEAR FROM MR. ROSS SOON.
BUT I AM NOT SO SURE.
I HAD HEARD, MR. HOLMES, THAT YOU ARE KIND TO POOR FOLK SO I CAME TO YOU AS QUICKLY AS POSSIBLE.

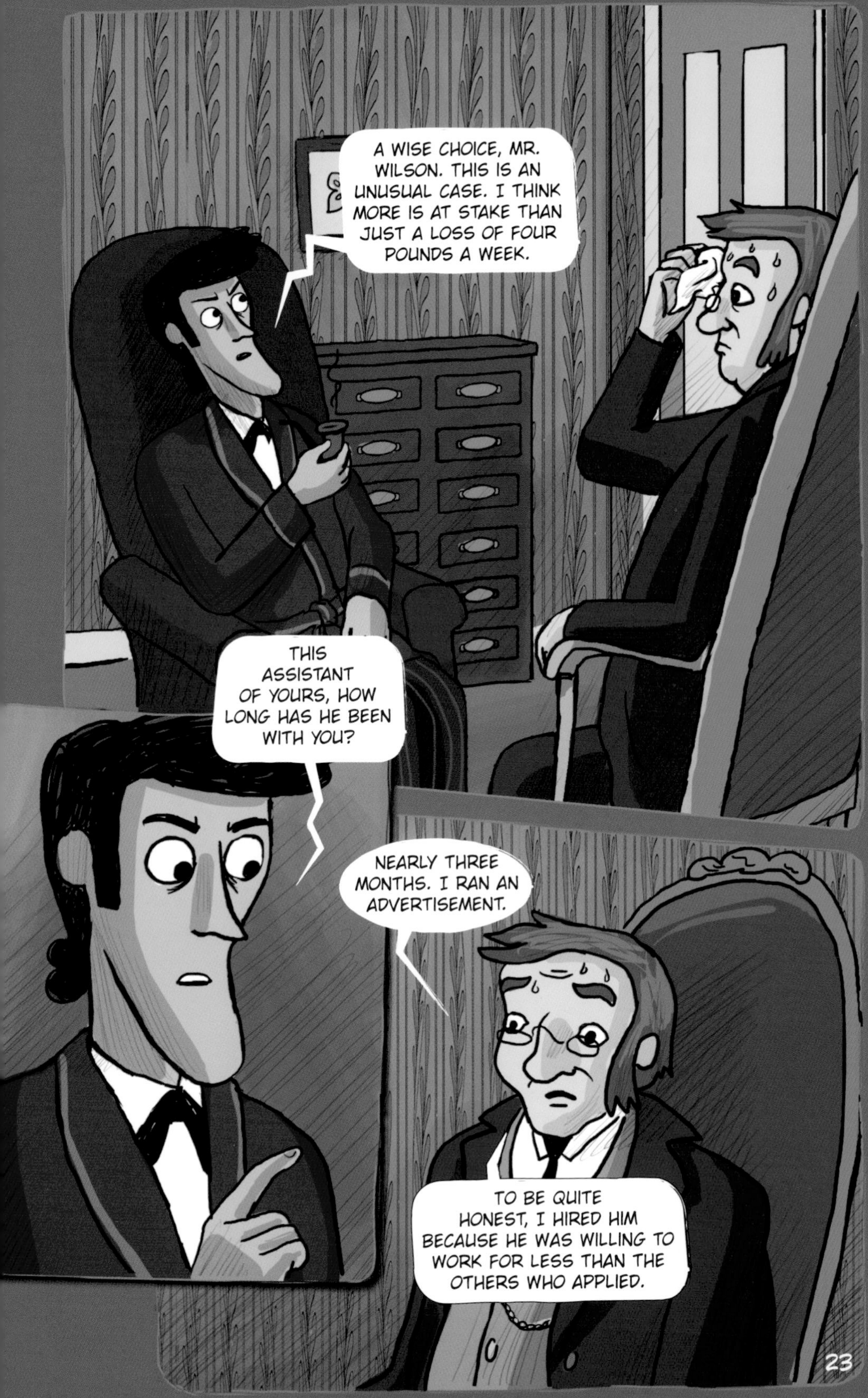
A WISE CHOICE, MR. WILSON. THIS IS AN UNUSUAL CASE. I THINK MORE IS AT STAKE THAN JUST A LOSS OF FOUR POUNDS A WEEK.
THIS ASSISTANT OF YOURS, HOW LONG HAS HE BEEN WITH YOU?
NEARLY THREE MONTHS. I RAN AN ADVERTISEMENT.
TO BE QUITE HONEST, I HIRED HIM BECAUSE HE WAS WILLING TO WORK FOR LESS THAN THE OTHERS WHO APPLIED.

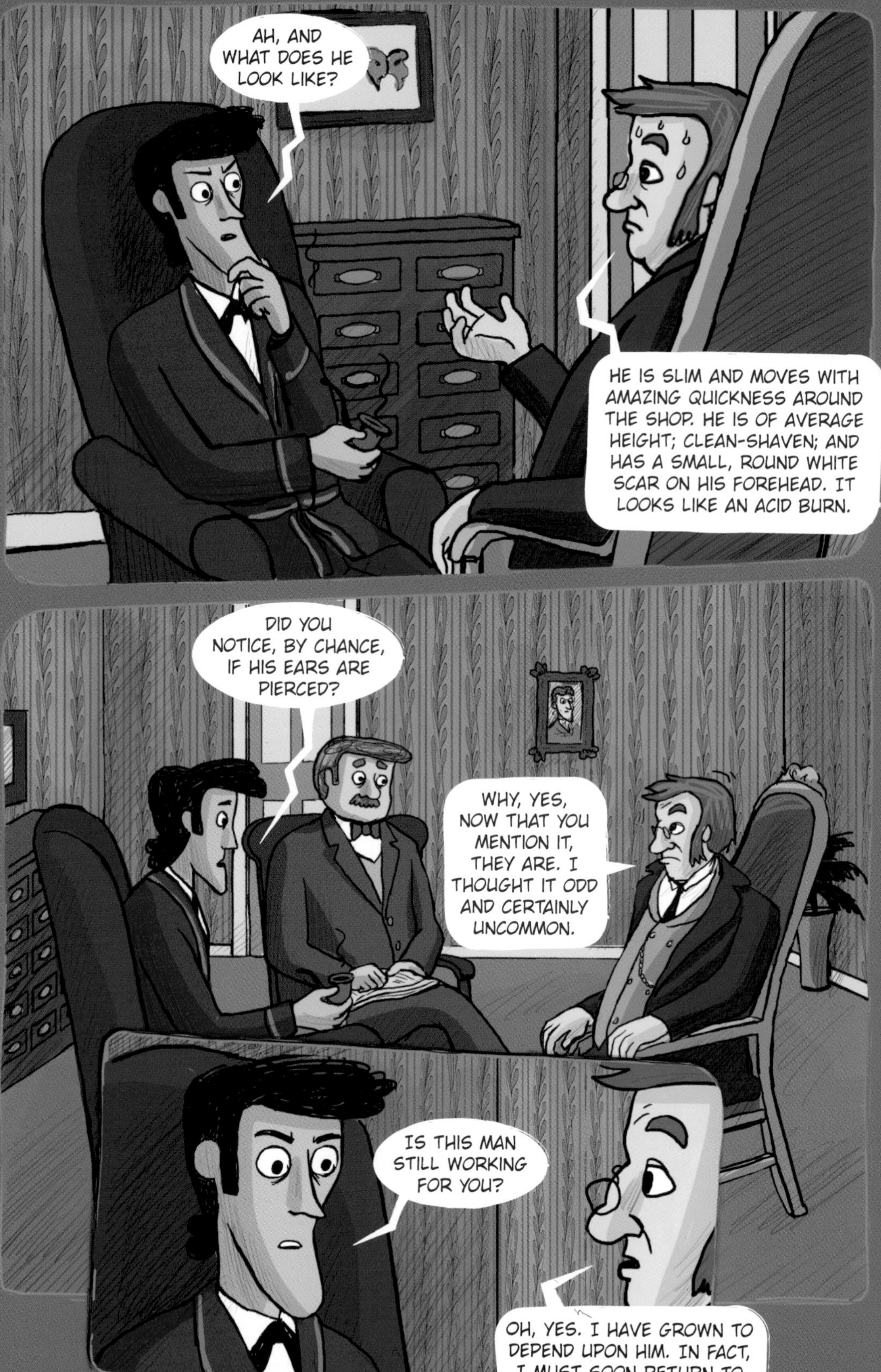
AH, AND WHAT DOES HE LOOK LIKE?
HE IS SLIM AND MOVES WITH AMAZING QUICKNESS AROUND THE SHOP. HE IS OF AVERAGE HEIGHT; CLEAN-SHAVEN; AND HAS A SMALL, ROUND WHITE SCAR ON HIS FOREHEAD. IT LOOKS LIKE AN ACID BURN.
DID YOU NOTICE, BY CHANCE, IF HIS EARS ARE PIERCED?
WHY, YES, NOW THAT YOU MENTION IT, THEY ARE. I THOUGHT IT ODD AND CERTAINLY UNCOMMON.
IS THIS MAN STILL WORKING FOR YOU?
OH, YES. I HAVE GROWN TO DEPEND UPON HIM. IN FACT, I MUST SOON RETURN TO ASSIST HIM.

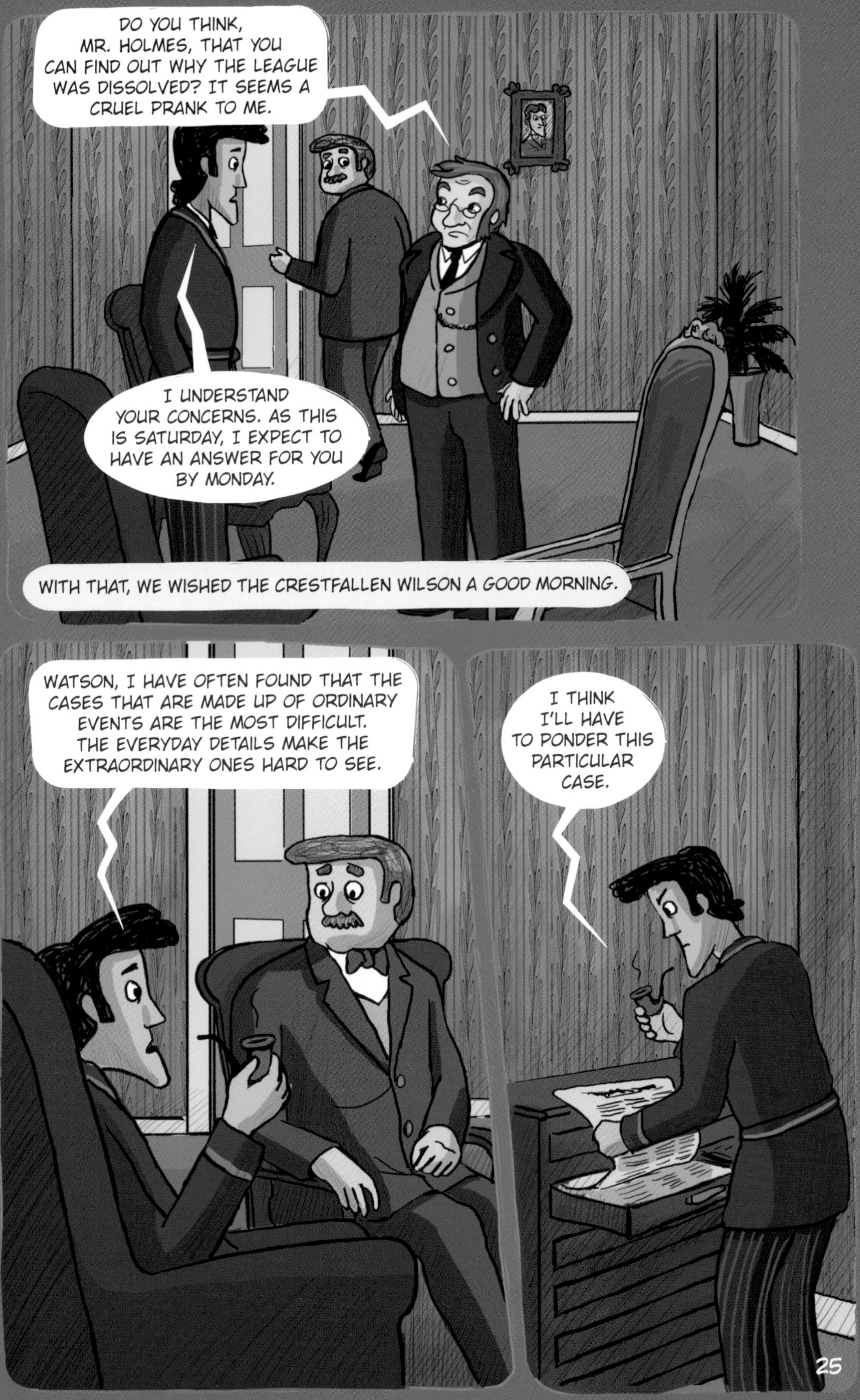
DO YOU THINK, MR. HOLMES, THAT YOU CAN FIND OUT WHY THE LEAGUE WAS DISSOLVED? IT SEEMS A CRUEL PRANK TO ME.
I UNDERSTAND YOUR CONCERNS. AS THIS IS SATURDAY, I EXPECT TO HAVE AN ANSWER FOR YOU BY MONDAY.
WITH THAT, WE WISHED THE CRESTFALLEN WILSON A GOOD MORNING.
WATSON, I HAVE OFTEN FOUND THAT THE CASES THAT ARE MADE UP OF ORDINARY EVENTS ARE THE MOST DIFFICULT. THE EVERYDAY DETAILS MAKE THE EXTRAORDINARY ONES HARD TO SEE.
I THINK I'LL HAVE TO PONDER THIS PARTICULAR CASE.

October 10, 1890 1:30 p.m.

Holmes shuffled through stacks and stacks of old newspaper articles he had saved. He seemed frustrated, so I stayed quiet and simply watched him. Every so often, he would pause and ponder for a moment before his attention again returned to the papers. Then, suddenly, he jumped to his feet, sending papers flying about the room. His eyes were sparkling.

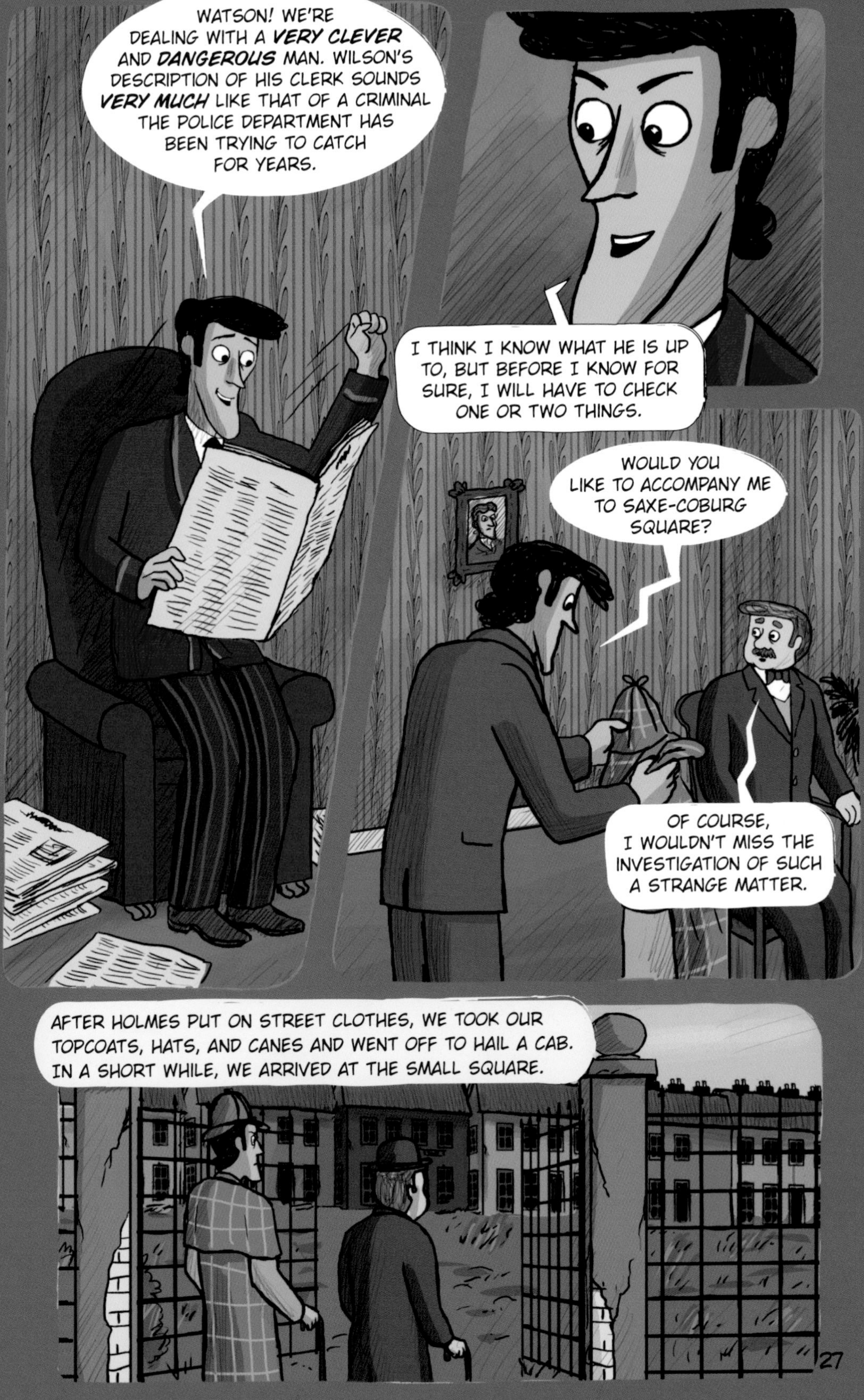
WATSON! WE'RE DEALING WITH A **VERY CLEVER** AND **DANGEROUS** MAN. WILSON'S DESCRIPTION OF HIS CLERK SOUNDS **VERY MUCH** LIKE THAT OF A CRIMINAL THE POLICE DEPARTMENT HAS BEEN TRYING TO CATCH FOR YEARS.
I THINK I KNOW WHAT HE IS UP TO, BUT BEFORE I KNOW FOR SURE, I WILL HAVE TO CHECK ONE OR TWO THINGS.
WOULD YOU LIKE TO ACCOMPANY ME TO SAXE-COBURG SQUARE?
OF COURSE, I WOULDN'T MISS THE INVESTIGATION OF SUCH A STRANGE MATTER.
AFTER HOLMES PUT ON STREET CLOTHES, WE TOOK OUR TOPCOATS, HATS, AND CANES AND WENT OFF TO HAIL A CAB. IN A SHORT WHILE, WE ARRIVED AT THE SMALL SQUARE.

Holmes approached Wilson's pawnshop and then walked up the street, peering at the buildings. When he reached the corner, he retraced his steps. As he neared the pawnshop entrance, he gave a few sharp raps on the pavement with his walking stick. I watched this little ritual with puzzled amusement. The pavement was old and dirty, but it sounded solid, not needing repair. Holmes smiled and rang the bell.

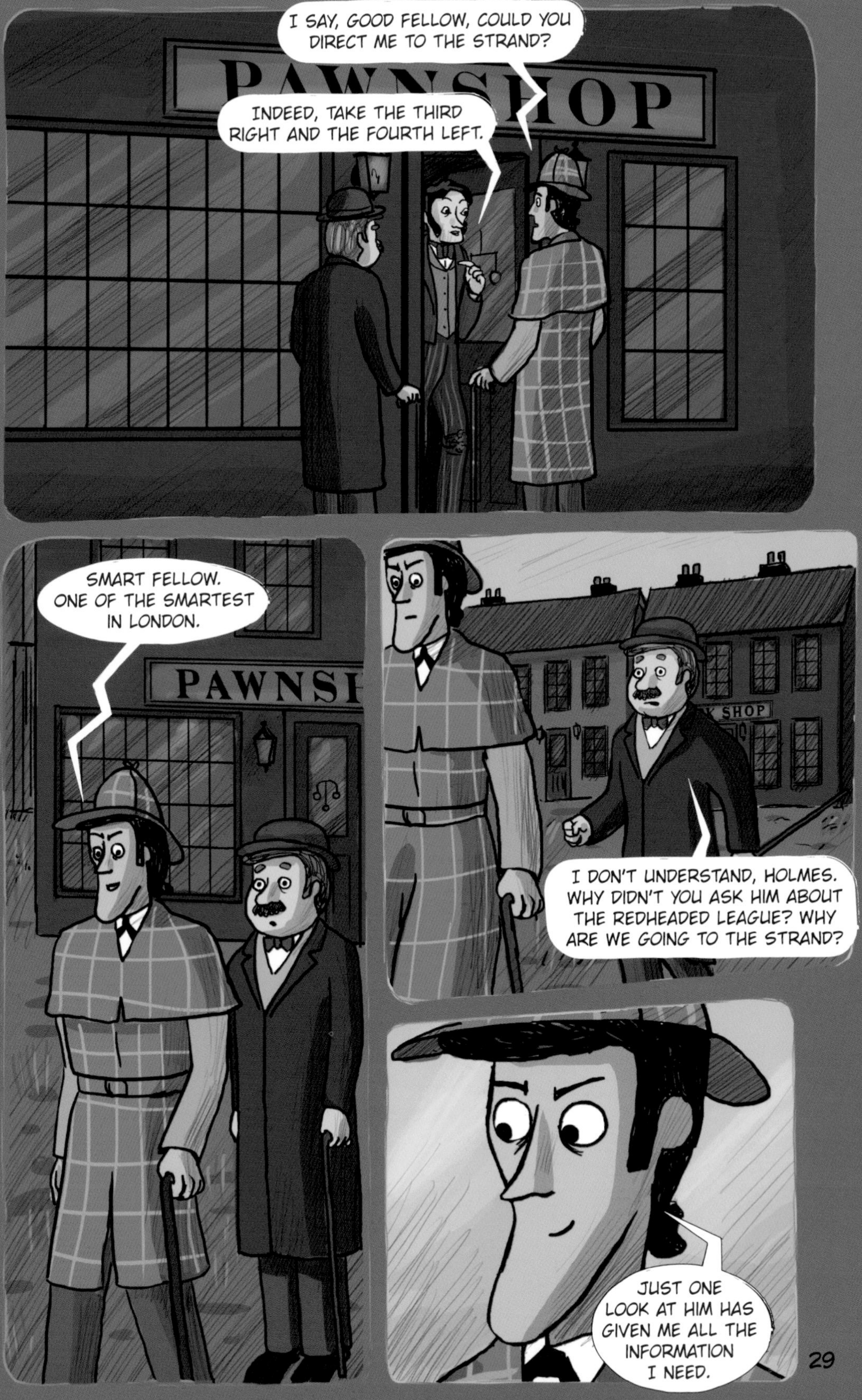

PAWNSHOP
I SAY, GOOD FELLOW, COULD YOU DIRECT ME TO THE STRAND?
INDEED, TAKE THE THIRD RIGHT AND THE FOURTH LEFT.
SMART FELLOW. ONE OF THE SMARTEST IN LONDON.
PAWNSH
I DON'T UNDERSTAND, HOLMES. WHY DIDN'T YOU ASK HIM ABOUT THE REDHEADED LEAGUE? WHY ARE WE GOING TO THE STRAND?
JUST ONE LOOK AT HIM HAS GIVEN ME ALL THE INFORMATION I NEED.

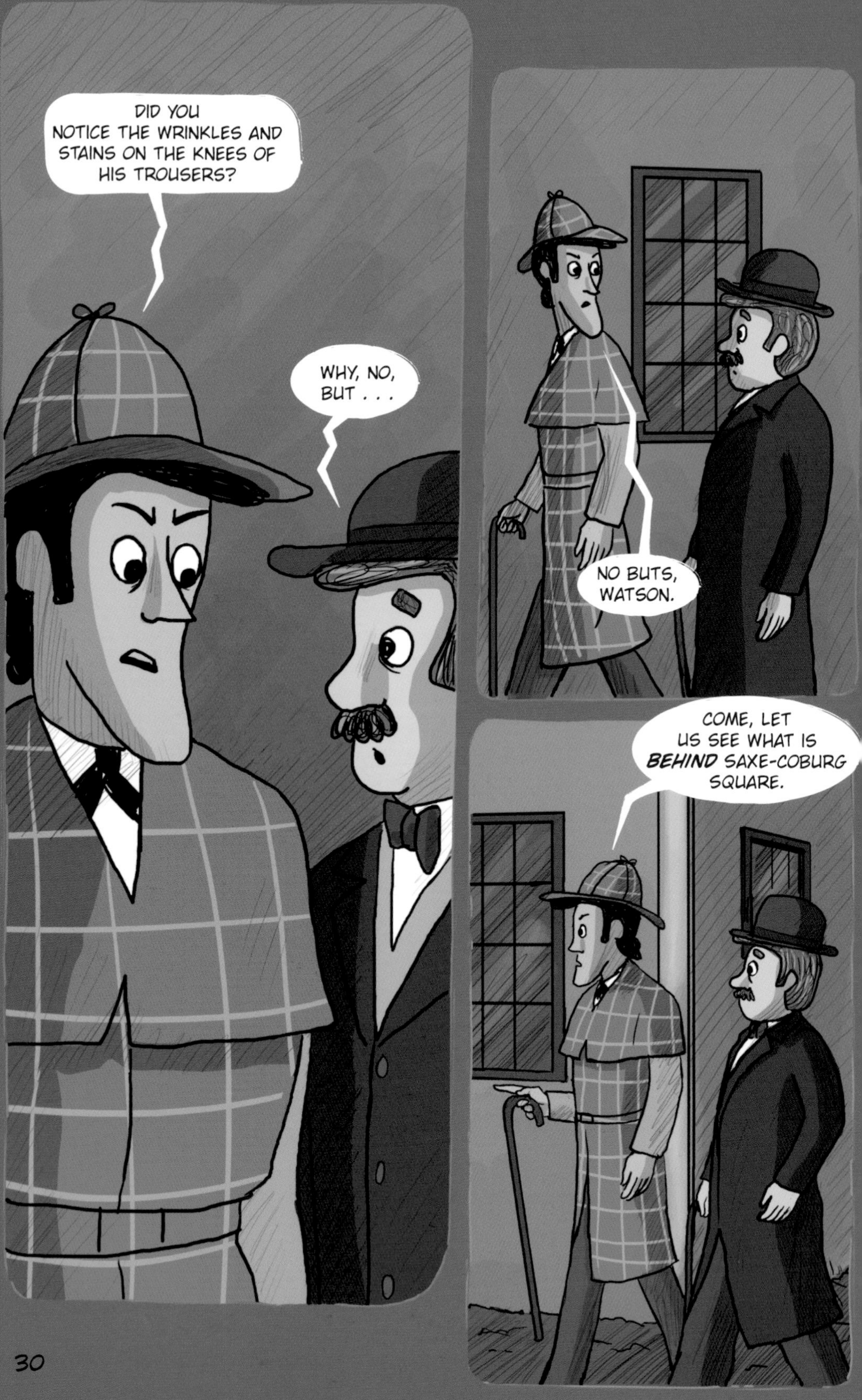
DID YOU NOTICE THE WRINKLES AND STAINS ON THE KNEES OF HIS TROUSERS?
WHY, NO, BUT . . .
NO BUTS, WATSON.
COME, LET US SEE WHAT IS BEHIND SAXE-COBURG SQUARE.

Holmes turned the corner and walked to the neighborhood behind the square. It was bustling with activity, unlike the quiet, forlorn little area we had just left. Here people were constantly passing. A steady stream of carriages and cabs was moving in both directions. Holmes carefully observed the buildings that were on either side of the busy street.

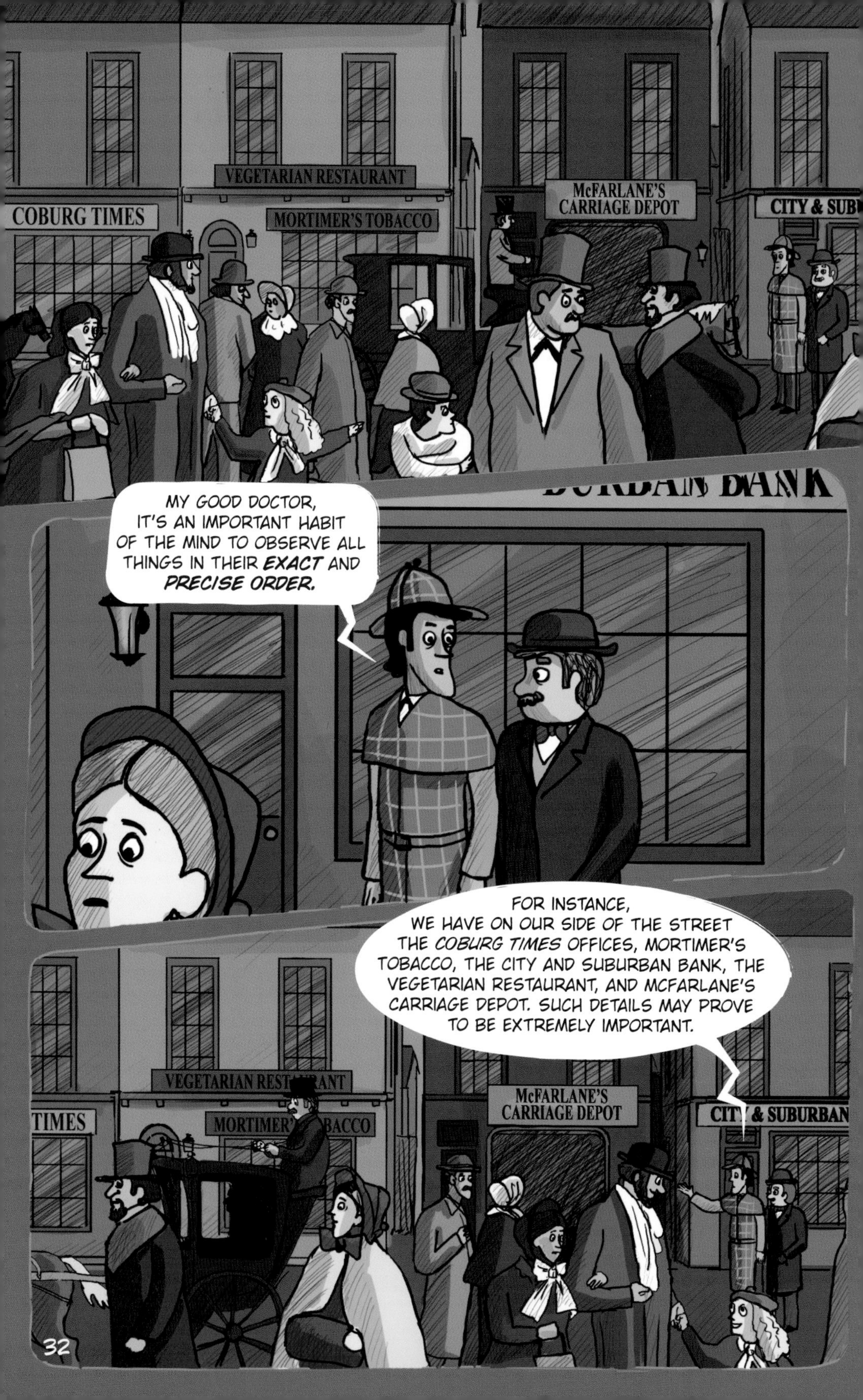

COBURG TIMES
VEGETARIAN RESTAURANT
MORTIMER'S TOBACCO
McFARLANE'S CARRIAGE DEPOT
CITY & SUB
BURBAN BANK
MY GOOD DOCTOR, IT'S AN IMPORTANT HABIT OF THE MIND TO OBSERVE ALL THINGS IN THEIR *EXACT* AND *PRECISE ORDER.*
FOR INSTANCE, WE HAVE ON OUR SIDE OF THE STREET THE *COBURG TIMES* OFFICES, MORTIMER'S TOBACCO, THE CITY AND SUBURBAN BANK, THE VEGETARIAN RESTAURANT, AND MCFARLANE'S CARRIAGE DEPOT. SUCH DETAILS MAY PROVE TO BE EXTREMELY IMPORTANT.
VEGETARIAN RESTAURANT
TIMES
MORTIMER'S TOBACCO
McFARLANE'S CARRIAGE DEPOT
CITY & SUBURBAN

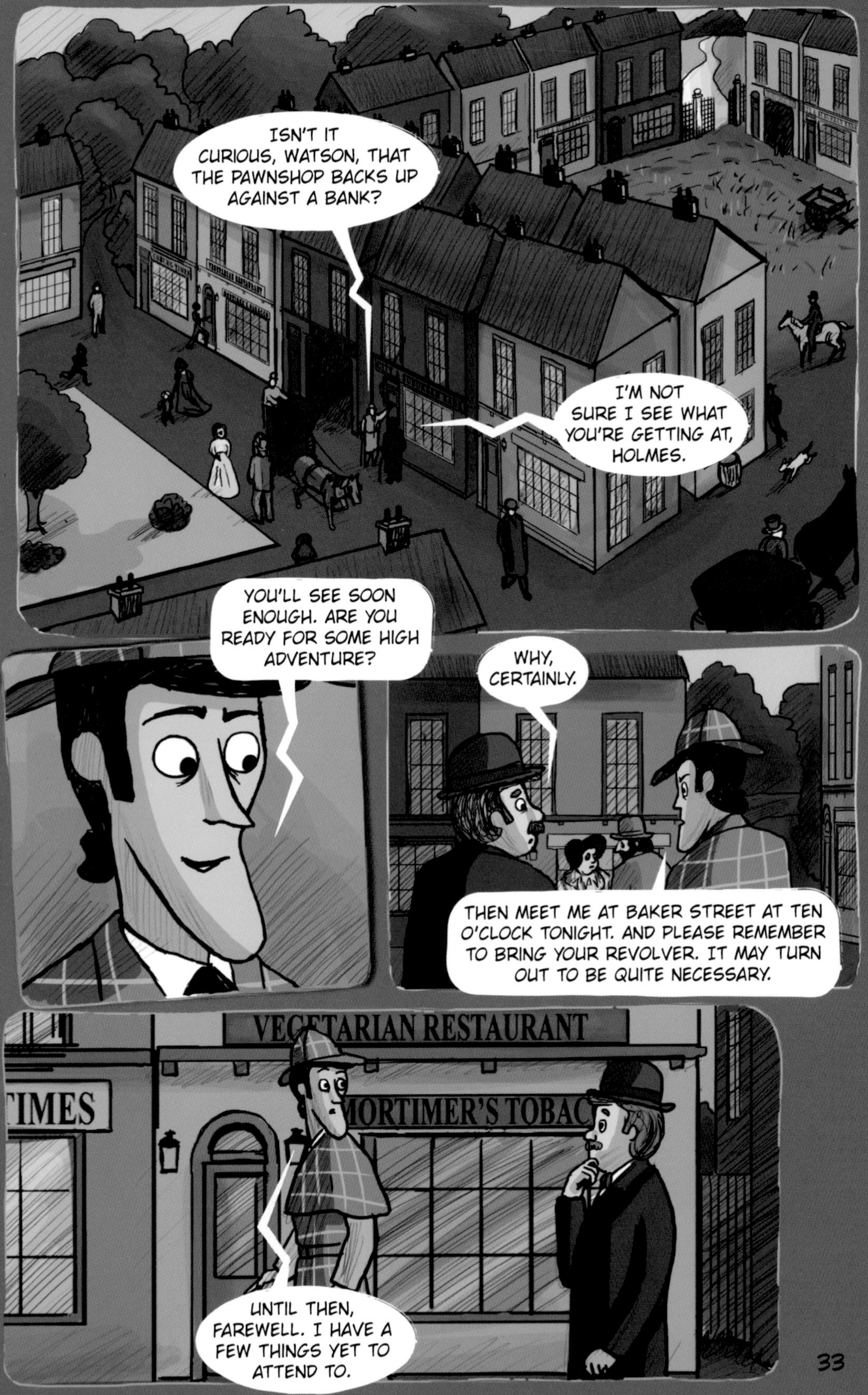
ISN'T IT CURIOUS, WATSON, THAT THE PAWNSHOP BACKS UP AGAINST A BANK?
I'M NOT SURE I SEE WHAT YOU'RE GETTING AT, HOLMES.
YOU'LL SEE SOON ENOUGH. ARE YOU READY FOR SOME HIGH ADVENTURE?
WHY, CERTAINLY.
THEN MEET ME AT BAKER STREET AT TEN O'CLOCK TONIGHT. AND PLEASE REMEMBER TO BRING YOUR REVOLVER. IT MAY TURN OUT TO BE QUITE NECESSARY.
VEGETARIAN RESTAURANT
TIMES
MORTIMER'S TOBAC
UNTIL THEN, FAREWELL. I HAVE A FEW THINGS YET TO ATTEND TO.

Holmes hailed a cab and left me pondering the whole situation. How could copying pages out of the *Encyclopaedia Britannica* lead to dangerous adventure? Where were we going tonight, and who were we fated to meet?

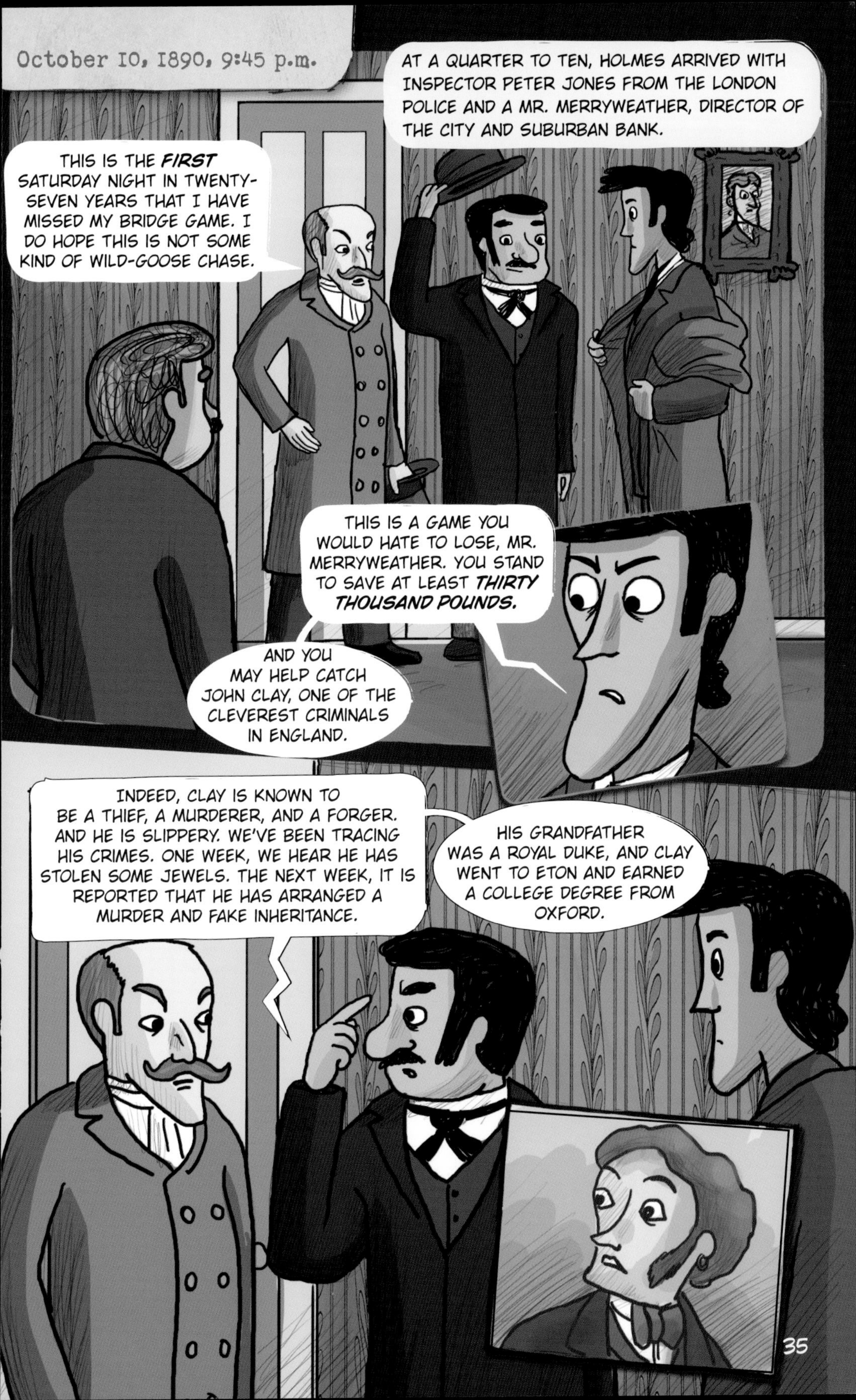
October 10, 1890, 9:45 p.m.
AT A QUARTER TO TEN, HOLMES ARRIVED WITH INSPECTOR PETER JONES FROM THE LONDON POLICE AND A MR. MERRYWEATHER, DIRECTOR OF THE CITY AND SUBURBAN BANK.
THIS IS THE *FIRST* SATURDAY NIGHT IN TWENTY-SEVEN YEARS THAT I HAVE MISSED MY BRIDGE GAME. I DO HOPE THIS IS NOT SOME KIND OF WILD-GOOSE CHASE.
THIS IS A GAME YOU WOULD HATE TO LOSE, MR. MERRYWEATHER. YOU STAND TO SAVE AT LEAST ***THIRTY THOUSAND POUNDS.***
AND YOU MAY HELP CATCH JOHN CLAY, ONE OF THE CLEVEREST CRIMINALS IN ENGLAND.
INDEED, CLAY IS KNOWN TO BE A THIEF, A MURDERER, AND A FORGER. AND HE IS SLIPPERY. WE'VE BEEN TRACING HIS CRIMES. ONE WEEK, WE HEAR HE HAS STOLEN SOME JEWELS. THE NEXT WEEK, IT IS REPORTED THAT HE HAS ARRANGED A MURDER AND FAKE INHERITANCE.
HIS GRANDFATHER WAS A ROYAL DUKE, AND CLAY WENT TO ETON AND EARNED A COLLEGE DEGREE FROM OXFORD.

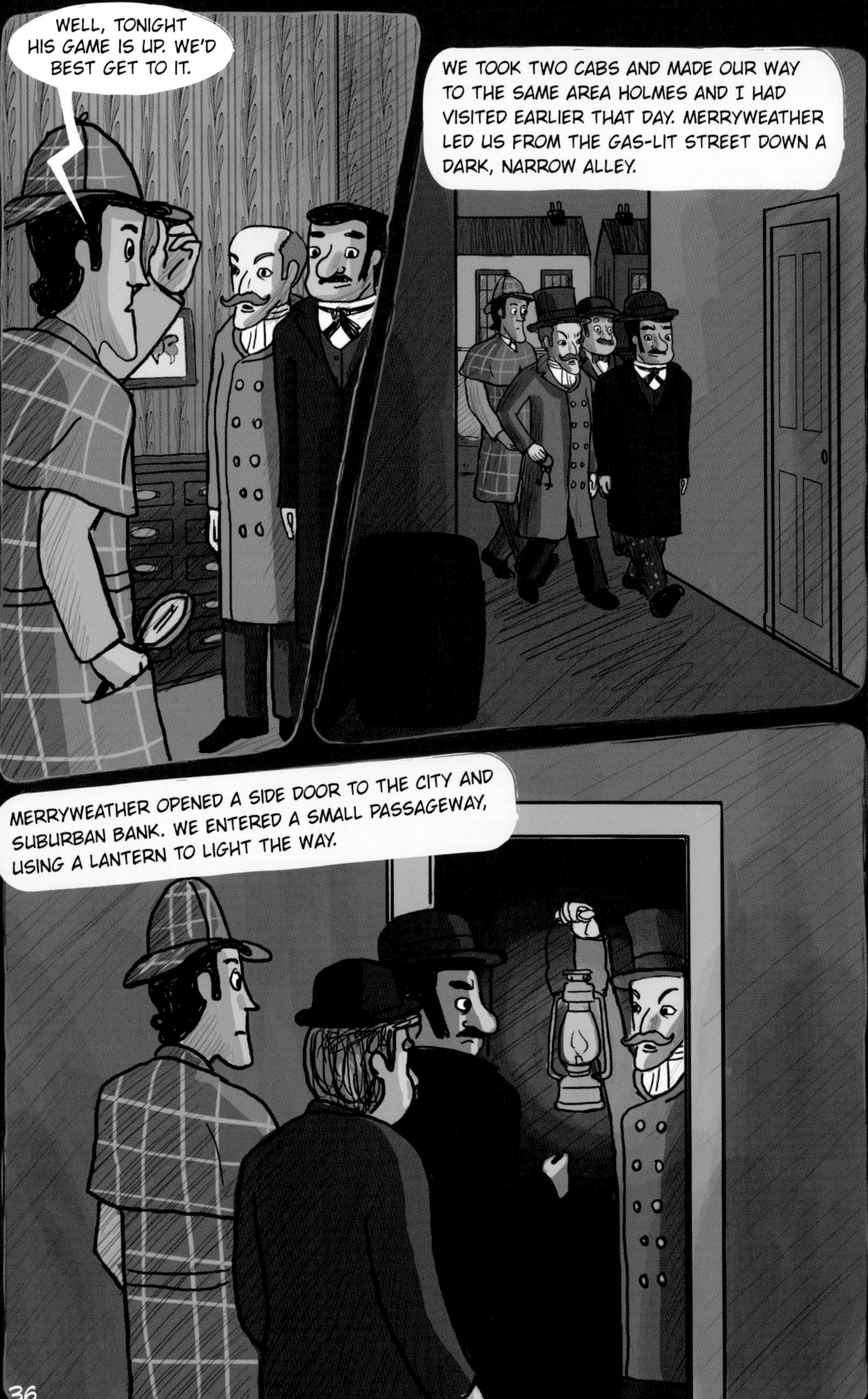
WELL, TONIGHT HIS GAME IS UP. WE'D BEST GET TO IT.
WE TOOK TWO CABS AND MADE OUR WAY TO THE SAME AREA HOLMES AND I HAD VISITED EARLIER THAT DAY. MERRYWEATHER LED US FROM THE GAS-LIT STREET DOWN A DARK, NARROW ALLEY.
MERRYWEATHER OPENED A SIDE DOOR TO THE CITY AND SUBURBAN BANK. WE ENTERED A SMALL PASSAGEWAY, USING A LANTERN TO LIGHT THE WAY.

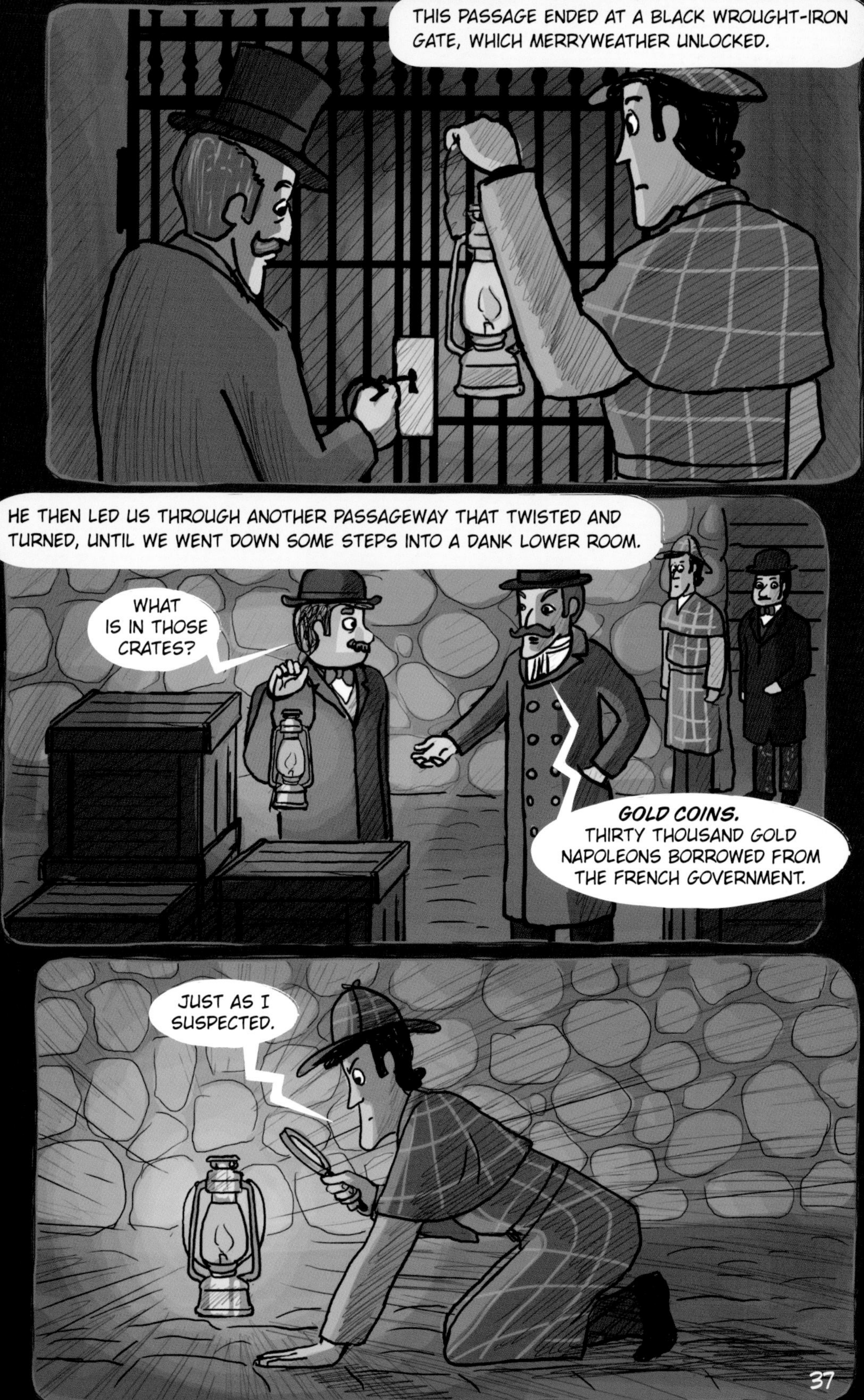
THIS PASSAGE ENDED AT A BLACK WROUGHT-IRON GATE, WHICH MERRYWEATHER UNLOCKED.
HE THEN LED US THROUGH ANOTHER PASSAGEWAY THAT TWISTED AND TURNED, UNTIL WE WENT DOWN SOME STEPS INTO A DANK LOWER ROOM.
WHAT IS IN THOSE CRATES?
GOLD COINS. THIRTY THOUSAND GOLD NAPOLEONS BORROWED FROM THE FRENCH GOVERNMENT.
JUST AS I SUSPECTED.

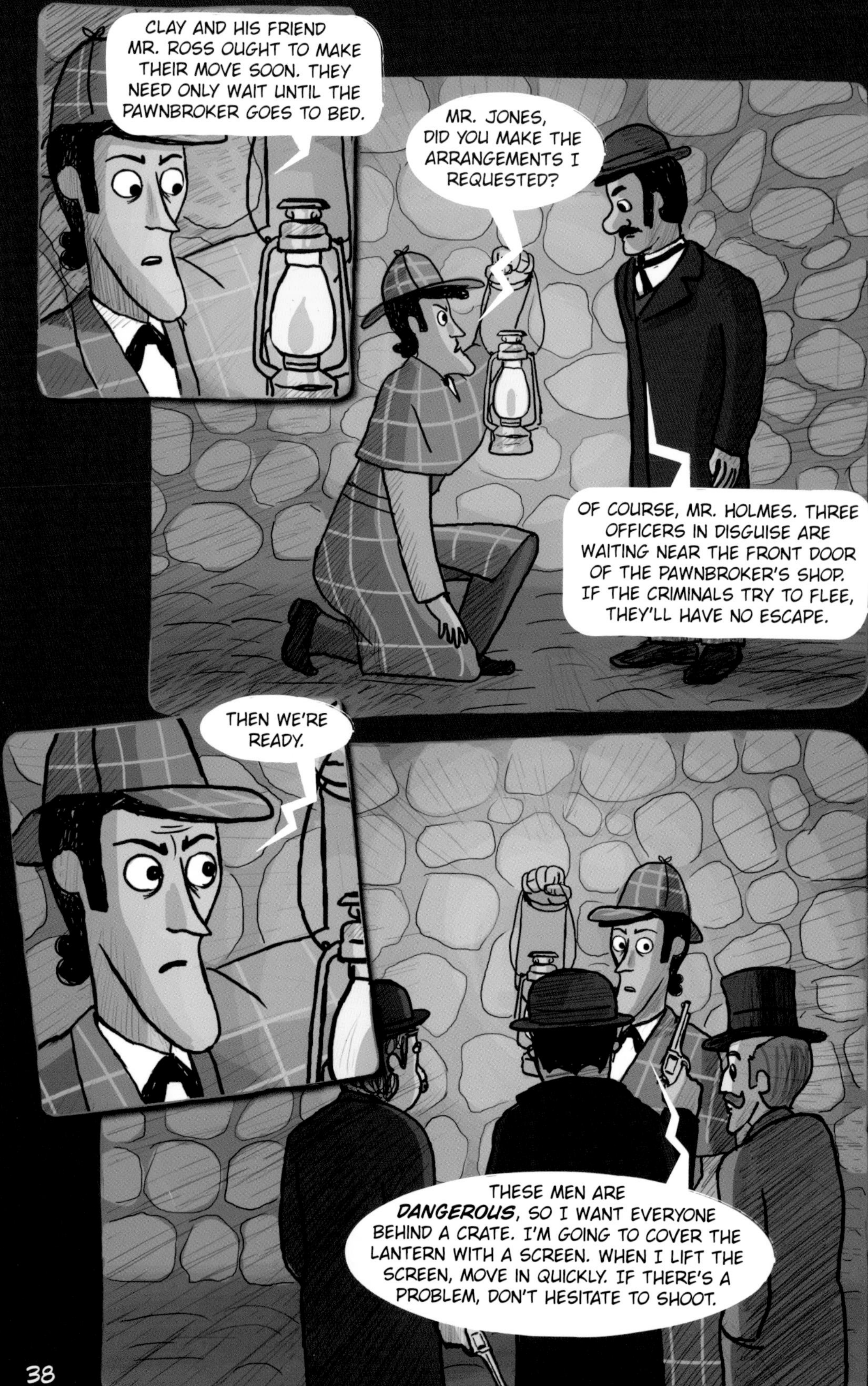
CLAY AND HIS FRIEND MR. ROSS OUGHT TO MAKE THEIR MOVE SOON. THEY NEED ONLY WAIT UNTIL THE PAWNBROKER GOES TO BED.
MR. JONES, DID YOU MAKE THE ARRANGEMENTS I REQUESTED?
OF COURSE, MR. HOLMES. THREE OFFICERS IN DISGUISE ARE WAITING NEAR THE FRONT DOOR OF THE PAWNBROKER'S SHOP. IF THE CRIMINALS TRY TO FLEE, THEY'LL HAVE NO ESCAPE.
THEN WE'RE READY.
THESE MEN ARE ***DANGEROUS***, SO I WANT EVERYONE BEHIND A CRATE. I'M GOING TO COVER THE LANTERN WITH A SCREEN. WHEN I LIFT THE SCREEN, MOVE IN QUICKLY. IF THERE'S A PROBLEM, DON'T HESITATE TO SHOOT.

We all took our positions, and Holmes covered the lantern. The darkness was complete, and the breathing of my companions seemed loud to my ears. My legs and knees grew sore from crouching, yet I dared not move lest I make a sound.

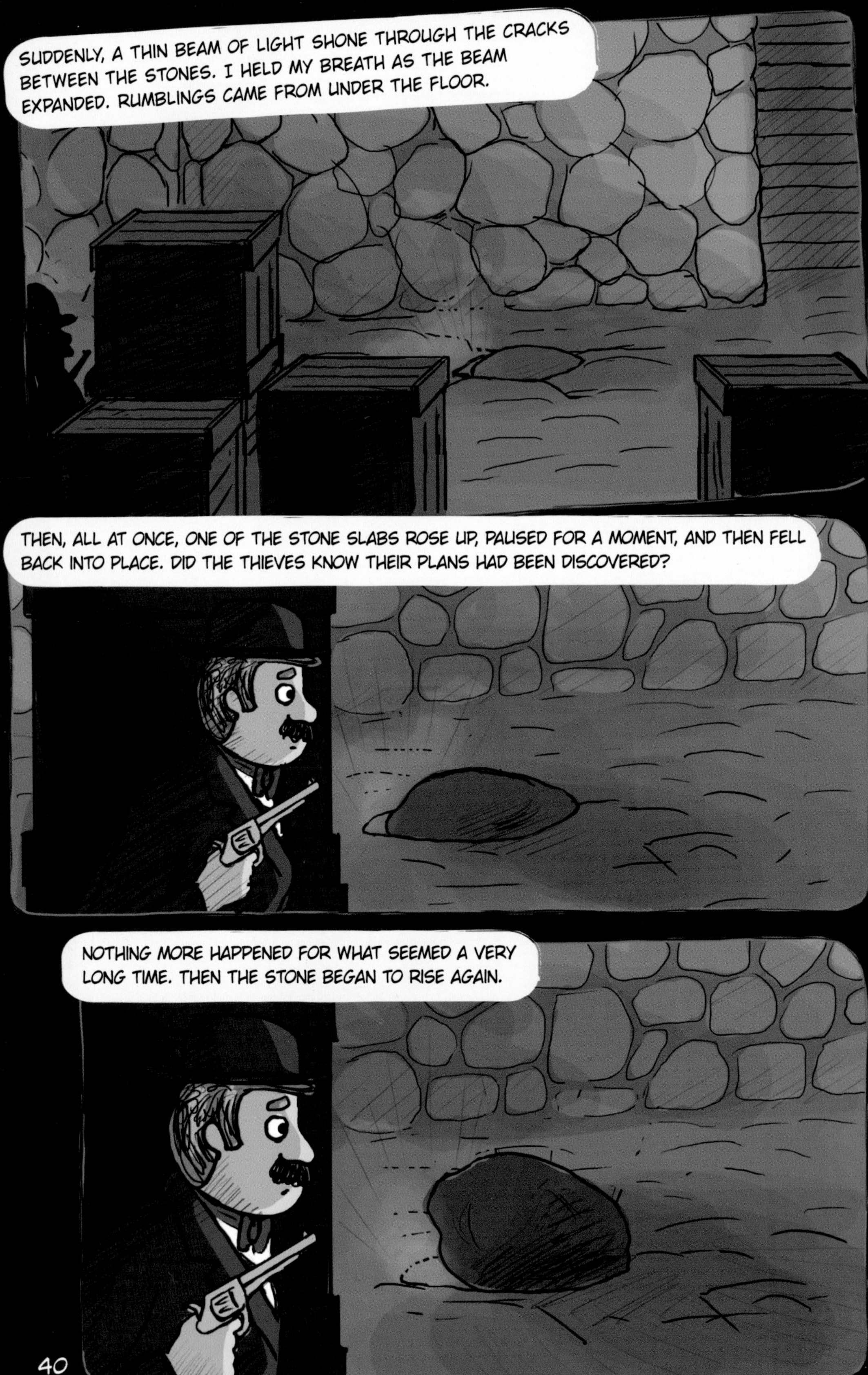
SUDDENLY, A THIN BEAM OF LIGHT SHONE THROUGH THE CRACKS BETWEEN THE STONES. I HELD MY BREATH AS THE BEAM EXPANDED. RUMBLINGS CAME FROM UNDER THE FLOOR.
THEN, ALL AT ONCE, ONE OF THE STONE SLABS ROSE UP, PAUSED FOR A MOMENT, AND THEN FELL BACK INTO PLACE. DID THE THIEVES KNOW THEIR PLANS HAD BEEN DISCOVERED?
NOTHING MORE HAPPENED FOR WHAT SEEMED A VERY LONG TIME. THEN THE STONE BEGAN TO RISE AGAIN.

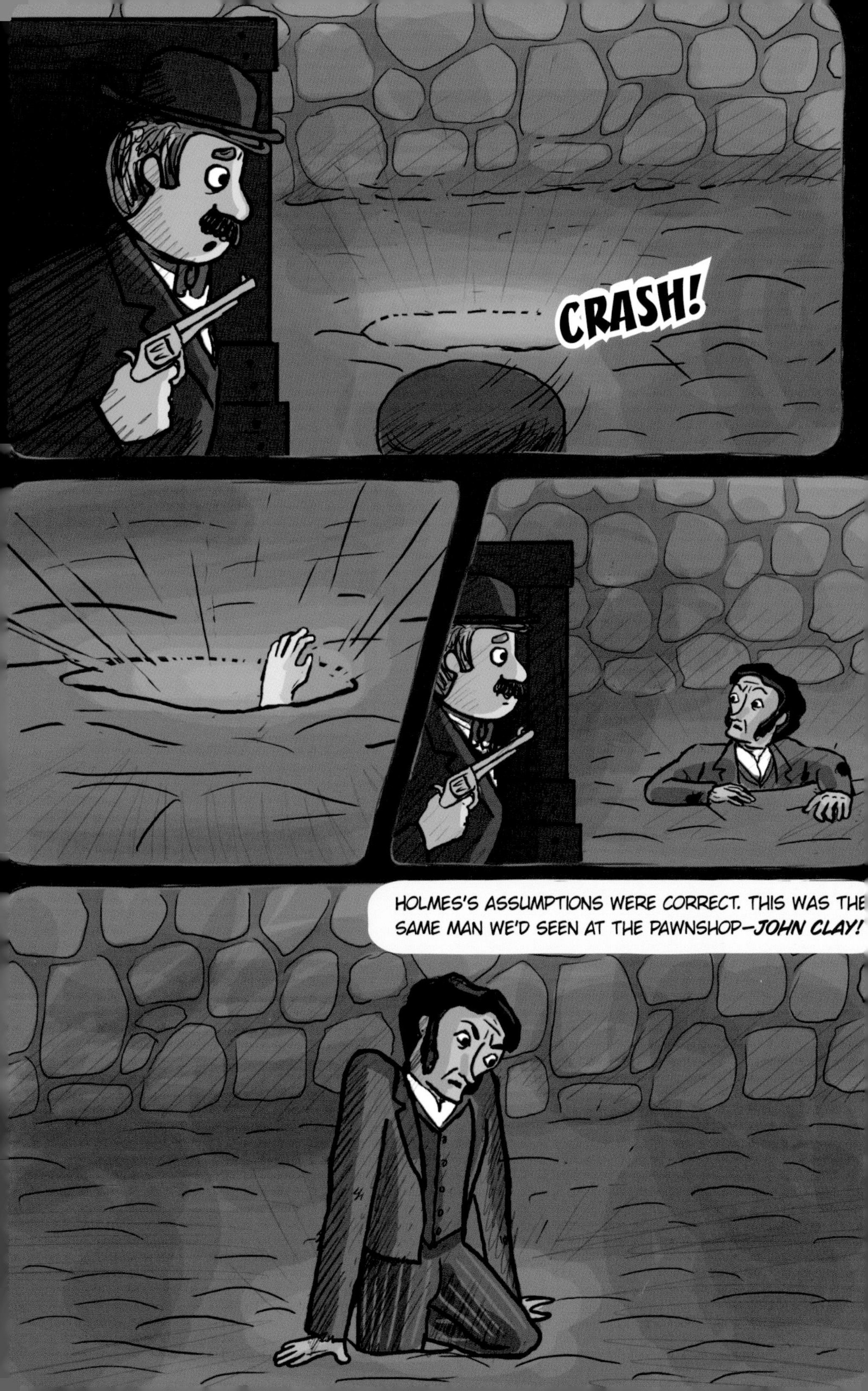
CRASH!
HOLMES'S ASSUMPTIONS WERE CORRECT. THIS WAS THE SAME MAN WE'D SEEN AT THE PAWNSHOP—JOHN CLAY!

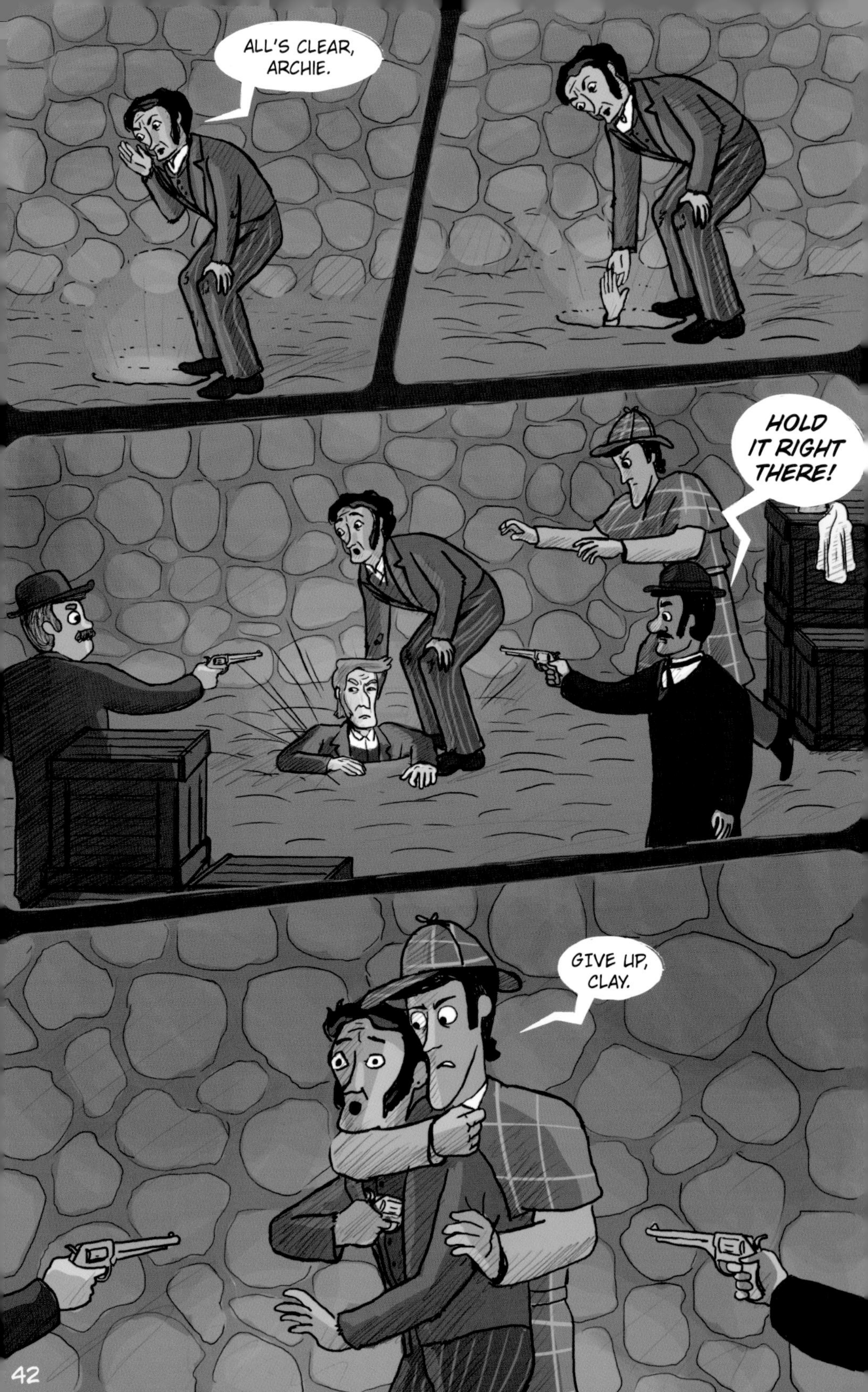
ALL'S CLEAR, ARCHIE.
HOLD IT RIGHT THERE!
GIVE UP, CLAY.

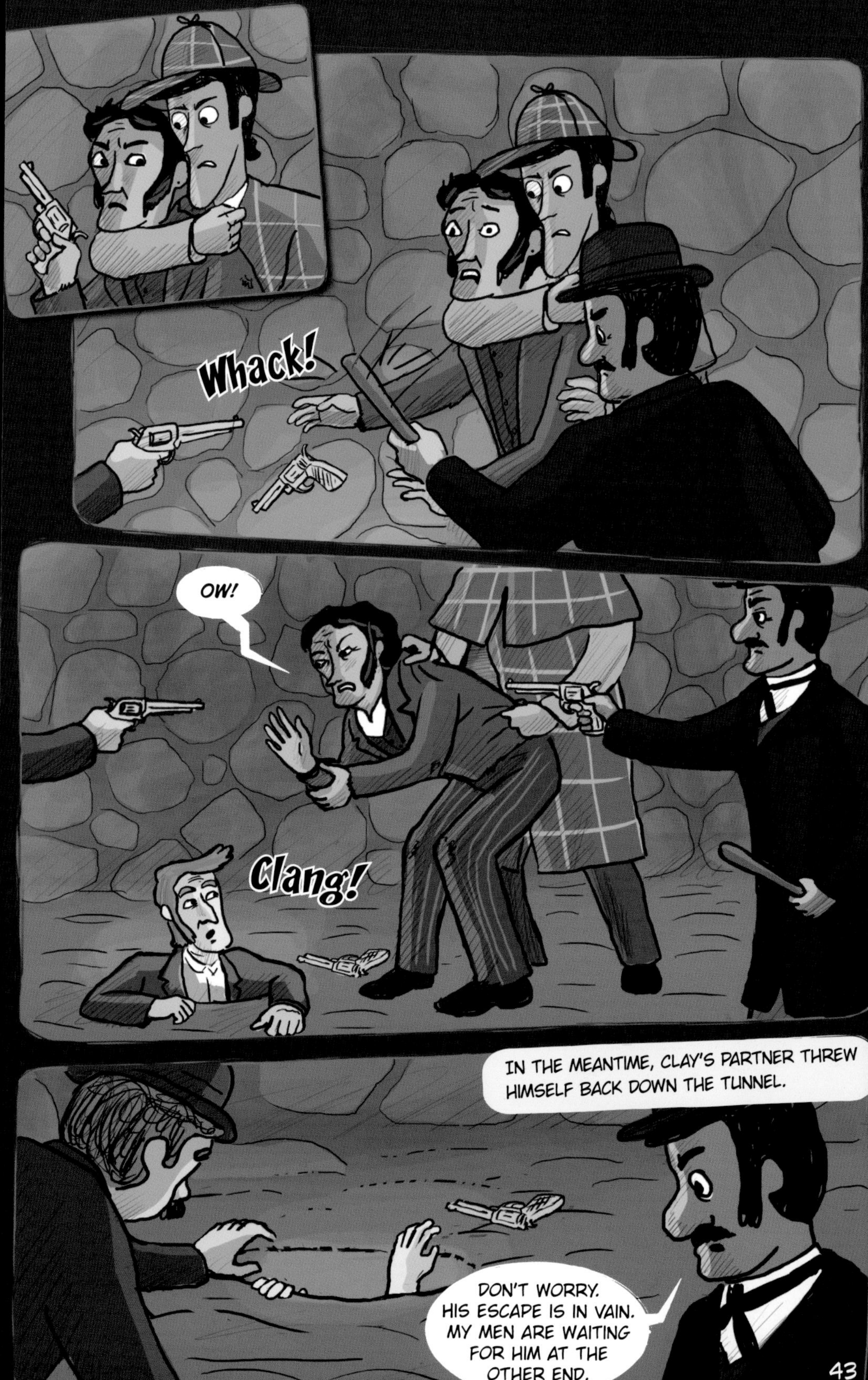
Whack!
OW!
Clang!
IN THE MEANTIME, CLAY'S PARTNER THREW HIMSELF BACK DOWN THE TUNNEL.
DON'T WORRY. HIS ESCAPE IS IN VAIN. MY MEN ARE WAITING FOR HIM AT THE OTHER END.

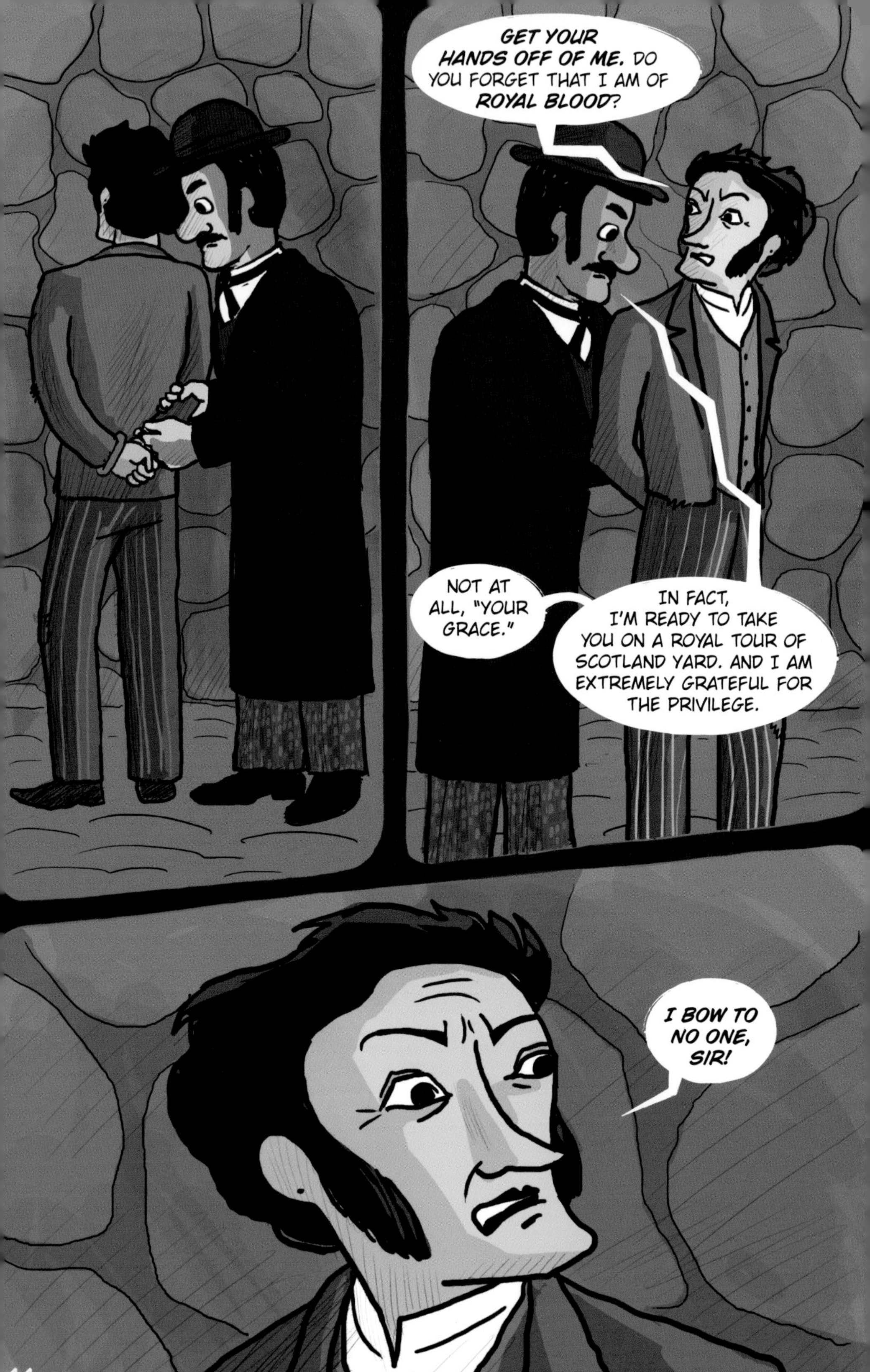
GET YOUR HANDS OFF OF ME. DO YOU FORGET THAT I AM OF ROYAL BLOOD?
NOT AT ALL, "YOUR GRACE."
IN FACT, I'M READY TO TAKE YOU ON A ROYAL TOUR OF SCOTLAND YARD. AND I AM EXTREMELY GRATEFUL FOR THE PRIVILEGE.
I BOW TO NO ONE, SIR!

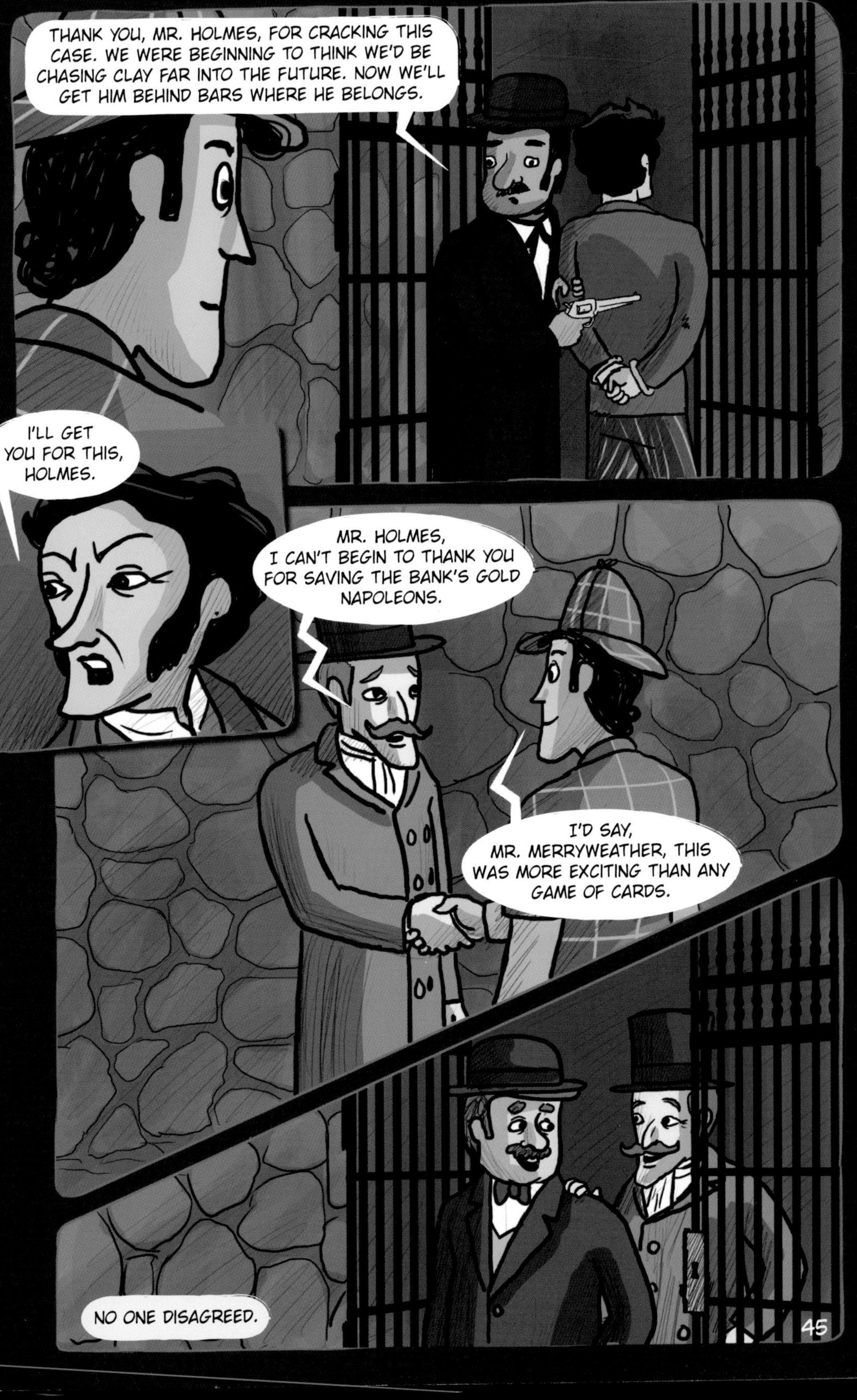
THANK YOU, MR. HOLMES, FOR CRACKING THIS CASE. WE WERE BEGINNING TO THINK WE'D BE CHASING CLAY FAR INTO THE FUTURE. NOW WE'LL GET HIM BEHIND BARS WHERE HE BELONGS.
I'LL GET YOU FOR THIS, HOLMES.
MR. HOLMES, I CAN'T BEGIN TO THANK YOU FOR SAVING THE BANK'S GOLD NAPOLEONS.
I'D SAY, MR. MERRYWEATHER, THIS WAS MORE EXCITING THAN ANY GAME OF CARDS.
NO ONE DISAGREED.

From the Desk of
John H. Watson, M.D.

The Redheaded League: How Did Holmes Solve It?

Why was Holmes suspicious of Wilson's clerk?

People don't usually agree to work for half wages. Holmes thought the clerk might have special reasons for wanting the job. The clerk must want to do something secret at the shop. This theory was strengthened by the fact that the clerk showed Wilson the advertisement for the Redheaded League. He clearly wanted Wilson to take the job outside the shop.

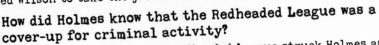

How did Holmes know that the Redheaded League was a cover-up for criminal activity?

Wilson's description of the Redheaded League struck Holmes as very strange. What purpose could there be in copying pages from the *Encyclopaedia Britannica*? Holmes thought the job with the Redheaded League must be a fake position.

How did Holmes suspect that the clerk was actually John Clay?

When Wilson mentioned that his clerk had an acid scar on his forehead, Holmes thought immediately of the notorious criminal John Clay. Clay had often been described in the newspapers.

How did Holmes confirm that the clerk was digging a tunnel?

Holmes thought the clerk's picture-taking habit was odd. It could be an excuse to go to the cellar. But what could be of interest in the cellar? A tunnel was the most likely explanation. This explanation was confirmed when Holmes saw the knees of the clerk's trousers. Obviously, he had been busy digging on his knees.

How did Holmes confirm the direction of the tunnel?

If there were a tunnel, it could go toward the square, to a neighboring house, or to something behind the shop. Holmes tapped on the pavement and found that it was solid. He knew then that there was no tunnel going toward the square. The tunnel must be headed for some place behind the shop. So Holmes checked out the neighborhood and found the bank.

How did Holmes know which night the criminals would complete their tunnel?

Since the Redheaded League had been dissolved, Holmes knew the tunnel was finished. Holmes reasoned that the thieves would seize the first possible evening to steal the gold. Their first chance would come that evening, when the bank was closed and the pawnbroker was asleep. If they succeeded, they would have Sunday and Monday to escape (banks in England are closed on those days). Holmes considered all this and made his plan accordingly.

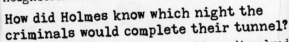

Further Reading and Websites

Baker's Street Journal
http://www.bakerstreetjournal.com

Barrett, Tracy. *The Case That Time Forgot.* New York: Henry Holt, 2010.

Brinley, Bertrand R. *The Mad Scientists' Club.* Keller, TX: Purple House Press, 2001.

Goodwin, Vincent. *The Adventure of the Red-Headed League.* Edina, MN: Magic Wagon, 2010.

Peacock, Shane. *The Secret Fiend: The Boy Sherlock Holmes, His Fourth Case.* New York: Tundra Books, 2010.

Sherlock Holmes Museum
http://www.sherlock-holmes.co.uk

Sir Arthur Conan Doyle Society
http://www.ash-tree.bc.ca/acdsocy.html

Springer, Nancy. *The Case of the Peculiar Pink Fan, An Enola Holmes Mystery.* New York: Puffin, 2010.

221 Baker Street
http://221bakerstreet.org

About the Author

Sir Arthur Conan Doyle was born on May 22, 1859. He became a doctor in 1882. When this career did not prove successful, Doyle started writing stories. In addition to the popular Sherlock Holmes short stories and novels, Doyle also wrote historical novels, romances, and plays.

About the Adapters

Murray Shaw's lifelong passion for Sherlock Holmes began when he was a child. He was the author of the Match Wits with Sherlock Holmes series published in the 1990s. For decades, he was a popular speaker in public schools and libraries on the adventures of Holmes and Watson.

M. J. Cosson is the author of more than fifty books, both fiction and nonfiction, for children and young adults. She has long been a fan of mysteries and especially of the great detective, Sherlock Holmes. In fact, she has participated in the production of several Sherlock Holmes plays. A native of Iowa, Cosson lives in the Texas Hill Country with her husband, dogs, and cat.

About the Illustrators

Sophie Rohrbach began her career after graduating in display design at the Chambre des Commerce in France. She went on to design displays in many top department stores including Galerias Lafayette. She also studied illustration at Emile Cohl school in Lyon, France, where she now lives with her daughter. Rohrbach has illustrated many children's books. She is passionate about the colors and patterns that she uses in her illustrations.

JT Morrow has worked as a freelance illustrator for over twenty years and has won several awards. He specializes in doing parodies and imitations of the Old and Modern Masters—everyone from da Vinci to Picasso. JT also exhibits his paintings at galleries near his home. He lives just south of San Francisco with his wife and daughter.